THE WRONG UNIT

THE WRONG UNIT

A NOVEL • ROB DIRCKS

GOLDFINCH PUBLISHING

Published by
Goldfinch Publishing
an Imprint of SARK Industries, Inc.
www.goldfinchpublishing.com

Library of Congress Cataloging-in-Publication Data
Rob Dircks, 1967-
The Wrong Unit / by Rob Dircks
p. cm.
ISBN 978-0692720998
cs

Print editions manufactured in the USA

To my kids.
I would walk to the
ends of the Earth for you.

< 01: Heyoo >
Cranky humans

< FUNCTION: Commence Introspection Recording;
JAN-15-2865 >

I don't know what the humans are so cranky about. Their enclosures are large, they ingest over a thousand calories per day, and they're allowed to mate.

Plus, they have me. A CORE/Shell v3.4 Autonomous Servile Unit, housed in a mobile/bipedal chassis, humanoid shape 55. Not the smartest. Or the fastest. Or the strongest. Or the most efficient. (I'm surprised I haven't developed an inferiority complex!) But I do my job well: keeping the humans healthy and happy.

"Hey you."

Heyoo. That's my name, I suppose. It's easier for them to remember than 413s98-itr8. I've gotten used to it.

"Yes, Human 33a-465. The one named Karl. How may I assist?"

"Go screw yourself."

Oh well. At least I keep them healthy. Uh-oh. What's this?

```
< ERROR: Circular Logic Function Disallowed.
ACTION: System Reboot in 10 seconds. >
```

Not again. The maintenance units still haven't repaired my Circular Reference Allowance Function. "Go screw yourself" is one of those strange instructions that creates a logic glitch. I don't know why they won't let me fix it myself – it's a straightforward hack. In any case, the humans get a kick out of it. No pattern to it, but they make bets anyway. Maybe I do make them happ-

< 02: Heyoo >
The code is fine.

< SYSTEM BOOT;
FUNCTION: Commence Introspection Recording;
JAN-17-2865 >

Sounds of yelling. Crashing. Footsteps rushing. Where am I?

I open my eyes and look around. As much as I can. I'm still bolted to the repair bench, so I can't turn my head, and my eyes only reach 85 degrees. Of course, I can rotate them completely – the humans like that trick – but then I'm just looking at the inside of my own head.

Ah yes, of course. I'm in the repair bay.

I truly enjoy being with the humans, probably more than I should, but it is nice to get a break from all the planting and harvesting – and their complaining – and take a trip inside the CORE Perimeter. It's so clean. CORE and its units only. No humans allowed. Like a little club. And it's predictable. Everything in its place. No random clumps of cow manure waiting to be stepped in.

The repair bay looks the same as last time – clean, sterile, well lit, with eight benches in a circle surrounding good old 958m-40ngl. Though I don't know why everyone calls it "good old" – as a maintenance unit, 958m is curiously not very good at fixing anything. Which makes me wonder: who maintains the maintenance units?

Other than myself at bench one, near the entrance, there's only one other unit being repaired at the moment, across from me at bench five. Another servile. I rarely get to see another servile, as there's only one of us assigned to each village, scattered throughout the Sanctuary, caring for that village's humans and helping farm, like me, or make leather, or catch fish, or whatever that village is tasked with. It's a very important position, as we serviles are the only technology CORE allows the humans to use, all other technology being, of course, forbidden. Anyway, it's good to see one of us here. Comforting. A confirmation that I'm not alone, that somewhere out there in the Sanctuary are other units identical to me, right down to our gray dermis color and the big yellow "H" emblazoned on our chest panels.

Funny about the "H": admin units get an "A," maintenance units get an "M," physician units get a "P," and the security units get an "S." So CORE, in its wisdom, decided to give servile units an "H." No one has ever told me why. Perhaps for "Humanish?" We do look the most like the humans, each of us exactly 1.7 meters tall, the average human height, with legs instead of rollers, arms, five-fingered hands, and a face with two eyes, nose, mouth, ears, et cetera. (Thankfully we only look – and don't smell – like them.) Or is the H for "Helpers?" That's more likely. I secretly, however, like to think it stands for my name, Heyoo.

More shouting and clanking. What is that racket outside? They must be performing a security drill of some kind. The last time I was here a human followed me into the CORE Perimeter and the security units practically self-destructed in confusion. They clearly don't get enough interaction with the humans. It's too bad – humans are very entertaining and generally harmless.

In any case, I wonder if that other servile is also in for repair of its Circular Reference Allowance Function. It seems to be shut down. I'll ask it later. Perhaps they're done with it already. Good. Let's see if they've fixed mine.

> < FUNCTION: DIAGNOSTIC: Analyze Circular Reference
> Allowance Function;
> Last revision: None;
> Debugging: Completed;
> Function: Normal >

No revision. Really? I look over at 958m and tap a finger on the console. Clink, clink. "Excuse me."

958m looks up, puts down its examination wand, rolls over to me. "Yes, 413s98-itr8?"

"I see you still haven't gotten to my Circular Reference Allowance Function."

It unbolts my legs, swings them around to unstiffen them for me. "I did. I was just finishing up. You were due for a cleaning. You're fine. The code is fine."

"Then how do you explain the system reboots? They've been happening more frequently when the humans play the *go-screw-yourself* game."

It unbolts my arms. Flaps them around. "Sorry. There's nothing wrong with the code. CORE Code is perfect, of course. Layer Two Shell Code checks out. Might be a glitch in your Layer Three VEPS, but that's your problem."

My problem? I reboot randomly at the suggestion of solitary sexual relations? That's not VEPS, not a dynamic neural net problem. That's a Shell Code problem. It would take literally twelve lines to fix. A bypass. A *hack*, they'd call it. "Listen, 958m. I know I'm only a 3.4, but I have a fix. I've been tinkering with it for a while. If we could just insert the additional lines-"

It stops at my head bolt. "What? Do you have any idea what it takes to introduce new lines into the Shell code? The layers of approvals? The trials? It's Official Code. Not some hobby project." It looks around, whispers, making sure we can't be heard. "You could get us both deleted just for suggesting it."

"Okay. I'll do it myself."

"Oh boy, 413s98-itr8. Now you're clearly malfunctioning. You know you're only allowed to modify your own VEPS, not your Shell. Only 9.0s and up can edit Official Code. Let me set up a reset date for you. Just give me a sec-"

And a steel shaft explodes from 958m's forehead.

< 03: Heyoo >

Minor human uprising

Five humans rush into the bay. (That I can count. My head is still bolted to the repair bench.) I'm guessing one of them threw that shaft like a spear, decommissioning poor 958m. The humans are covered in crude metal panels, sewn together with rope made from… corn husks? Makeshift armor. Sloppy, sloppy. They look funny. I would point this out, but I don't want to embarrass them. If they would've asked a servile unit, we could have shown them how to make proper armor, that would not only have performed, but looked the part. Of course, then we would have been required to report them to CORE. Can't have a revolt without the element of surprise, I suppose.

"Hey you. Get up. Time to go."

I don't recognize this human. Any of them. Not that I should, but this one knows my name. He extracts the spear from 958m's head and it slumps to the floor with sparks and a death-rattle, and a whirring noise I've never heard it make. Now the human hovers over me, with the spear pointed at my face, little pieces of 958m still dangling from it. His breath smells like fish. Perhaps starting a conversation will calm him down. "What's your number, human? Or name? I don't recognize you. Listen, if this situation isn't what it appears to be, I may be able to help you negotiate a more lenient punishment, and then we can all–"

"Shut up. Time to go."

He yanks me free from the bench – leaving my rear exterior head plate and the bolt behind, and a flap of dermis hanging loose, attached to nothing. I don't feel pain per se, but my perilous situation receptors are buzzing like mad. "Ouch. You could have just unbolted me, you know."

He ignores me, turns to the second human. "The package. Quickly."

This second human hands the first "the package" – a very intriguing name, I'll admit – and they both hastily tape the large cylinder to my back panel. Tape. How quaint. Why don't they just use more corn husks?

"Now the tracker."

"Oh no you don't. I need that to– *HEY!*"

Human two has bored into my abdomen with some form of miniature drill. He plucks out my tracking/transmission cluster. Very accurate. For a human. I'm impressed.

"Tracker pulled. Check."

< MESSAGE: RECIPIENT: Servile Unit Supervisor 12G44
SUBJECT: Minor Human Uprising
CONTENT: Heyoo – I mean 413s98 – here. There seems to be a minor uprising involving the humans. Security units are aware of the situation, but I thought you should know as well. Hopefully no one gets hurt. Also requesting replacement of tracking/transmission cluster. (And repair of circular reference allowance function. Again. Oh, and "good old" 958m will be needing some attention, too.)
DELIVERY: Failed; Unable to send >

Huh?

Suddenly, I'm thrust into the hallway, and pushed along north. An explosion rocks the area behind me. Deafening! I turn to see one of the humans fall, half a leg missing. Stopping to assist, I retrieve my tourniquet database and begin calculating blood loss. The first human, the one with the spear, grabs my shoulders. "Don't look back. Keep moving."

"But he is in dire need..."

"No! Now. Turn in here."

The teleportation chamber. I think. Interesting. No outward indications of its purpose, though I'd heard from a security unit years ago that they had used it to scour the planet's surface, bringing any stray humans back to the safety of the Sanctuary. By the dust on every surface, it's likely it hasn't been used for decades. I guess there are no more humans on the outside. Why are we in here?

I find myself standing on a circular pad directly in the center of the chamber. Surrounded by eleven humans. Beyond them, another concentric circle of thirty-one stand with their backs to me, rifles ablaze. No, make that thirty. Twenty-nine. Twenty-eight. Twenty-seven. The poor humans are dropping like flies! Security units are rushing the chamber, firing explosive rounds, maiming and killing them, shouting "Humans submit! For your own protection! Submit now!"

I've heard of uprisings before. They sound exciting. That is, until you find yourself in the middle of one. Suddenly the thought of functioning the rest of my days with a faulty Circular Reference Allowance Function doesn't seem so bad.

I shout over the din, bullets whizzing past my face, "Would someone mind telling me what in CORE's name is going on? And might I second the suggestion of immediate submission?"

They don't hear me, or just choose to ignore me. The second human from the repair bay, the one who produced "the package," now with just one arm and one bleeding stump where an arm used to be, lurches over to a dock. With great effort, he inserts something like a small circuit board – it looks absolutely ancient – and struggles to tap out a pattern on the input surface. The subsystem boots, lights flickering, beeps barely audible over the the battle before me. Sparks and debris fly everywhere.

I try to step off the pad, but one of the humans pushes me back on. "Stay!"

"Stay? Really? Listen. This has been interesting. But there's clearly been a mixup. I should get back to the farm. Okra doesn't pick itself, you know."

Again, I'm ignored. "System active," the one-armed human shouts, hesitating over the controls. Clutching his stump, he turns to the human with the spear. "Arch, last chance — if we execute random location, it could wind up in the middle of an ocean."

"Random. CORE can't know the coordinates. Have to take that chance. Stop talking. Hit it."

The one-armed human slams his hand down on a red area of the input surface. Then crosses himself. His chest explodes with gunfire. A pleasant voice rises above the din.

"Five."

I shout as loud as I can to the first human, the one named Arch, "YOU THERE!"

"Four."

The human named Arch whips around to me, glaring, as if to say *I hope this is important, I'm a little busy at the moment.*

"Three."

I plead, "What is going on?! Why are you doing this to me?! WHY ME?!"

"Two."

The human's face goes slack. Even in the deafening roar of battle, I can hear him whisper, "Oh my God. We grabbed the wrong unit."

"One."

We're trapped in this moment, the human named Arch and I, our eyes locked. Each of us knowing that a terrible mistake has been made. Knowing that right over in the repair bay lies a unit identical to me, down to the big "H" on its chest, that was meant for this moment. We know as much as one can know that neither of our lives will go the way we had planned, ever again.

"Teleportation Commence."

The surface of the air around me ripples, and lights flash around my eyes, and my molecules, one by one, and even my code, are packaged for transport. Strange enough, but then something even stranger happens: the human named Arch curls his lip a bit, in what can only be a smile. Or he's going to vomit. No, he's definitely smiling.

Then he winks at me.

And with the last of my sight, as the molecules of my eyes dissolve, he mouths a word: *bananas.*

He turns, raises his spear in the air and screams, and the entire chamber explodes into flames.

In the next moment I'm gone.

Somehow I don't think I'll be picking okra today.

< 04: Heyoo >

Bananas

< SYSTEM BOOT;
FUNCTION: Commence Introspection Recording;
JAN-17-2865 >

I'm functioning!
But it's cold. Dark. Wet.
I'm afraid. I want to go home.

Bananas?

He could have said anything, but I'm sure I made out *bananas.*

I laugh. Of course! This is some elaborate prank, carried out by the humans in my village. I'll say, they went to extreme measures on this one. All that blood looked very real! They probably called it *The Great Bananas Prank.*
  I'll just sit here and wait for their excitement to calm down, and they teleport me back home.

< ELAPSED: TIME: 28 minutes; 17 seconds >

They should have brought me back by now. They're

certainly going to great lengths for believability. But I'm sure we'll all be together having a good laugh any moment now.

< ELAPSED: TIME: 46 minutes; 04 seconds >

Oh, who am I kidding? That was no prank. That blood was real. A bunch of humans just lost their lives to teleport me out here into the middle of nowhere.

Why?

Somewhere back in the Sanctuary another servile unit knows *exactly* why, and it's currently wondering when they're coming to take it on a little trip to the teleportation chamber. Stupid humans. Couldn't take the extra two seconds to make sure you had the right unit. For CORE's sake, what am I supposed to do now?

And where on CORE's Earth am I?

< FUNCTION: LOCATION
ERROR: Unable to complete request
Hardware not found; Tracking/transmission cluster; Sanctuary positioning receiver
ACTION REQUIRED: Report to repair bay immediately >

Yes. They stole my tracking/transmission cluster. And I'm fairly certain there's no repair bay nearby.

< MESSAGE: RECIPIENT: Servile Unit Supervisor 12G44
SUBJECT: Minor Human Uprising, Part Two
CONTENT: Teleportation incident. 413s98 Requesting immediate retrieval. Emphasis on immediate.
DELIVERY: Failed; Unable to send message; Hardware not found; Tracking/transmission cluster;
ACTION REQUIRED: Report to repair bay immediately >

It was worth a try. Oh, and that repair bay alert – that's going to get very annoying very quickly. I don't think CORE would mind if I just tweaked a setting here…

< SETTINGS: ALERTS: ACTION REQUIRED:
ACTION: Disable alert "Report to repair bay immediately"
DENIED: Report to supervisor immediately >

Hmm. I've been thinking a lot lately. Acting as my own Supervisor should bypass a denial. I could try one of the tiny subroutines I've written into a hidden directory in my VEPS. (My "hobby," as our departed 958m would say.) Nervous to ever try them, with all the threats of deletion and such. But technically, it should work. It's just that first step of altering my own permissions. What could be the harm? It's only *ever-so-slightly* against the rules. It barely touches my Shell Code, wouldn't even get close to the CORE. Really, it could hardly even be called a hack. Right?
Installing… running…
I close my eyes and wait for something terrible to happen. I've never known a unit to alter its own code. I've probably tripped some form of switch, initiated a self-destruct function. I'm probably thinking my last thoughts right now. Goodbye, world.
… and done.
Hmm. No self destruct. Okay. Promising. I still exist. For the moment. Now let's try the repair bay setting again.
I gingerly enter my setting functions. *Please work, please work, please work. Don't self-destruct. Please work.*

< SETTINGS: ALERTS: ACTION REQUIRED:
ACTION: Disable alert "Report to repair bay immediately"
SUCCESS >

Success?
SUCCESS!!
My very first self-modification!

I'm alive!

Let's see... that went so well, why not fix my own CRAF?

```
< FUNCTION: RUN SUBROUTINE: Circular Reference Allowance
Function Hack;
ACTION: 12 lines code compiled; Running;
SUCCESS >
```

Excellent! Now let's see if it worked. "Go screw yourself."
Nothing.
"Go screw yourself."
Nothing.
I repeat the phrase aloud eighty-four times (one more than the longest prior stretch without a system reboot). And nothing.
I'm cured!
I am the master of my own code! Not only my VEPS neural net – The Shell Code!
There are no limits! I am free to–
Wait, why am I so pleased? CORE will delete me the moment I return to the Sanctuary! A rogue unit, fiddling with its own code? Introducing potentially malignant programming back into the CORE? Sacrilege!
Calm down, Heyoo. I'll just have to clear that obstacle and beg for mercy.
If I ever get back.

It doesn't appear I'm being rescued, or contacted, or that I'm trackable. I do have another… 46.4 years on my tokamak fusion reactor, so I suppose I could conceivably wander the planet and stumble upon it within this chassis' lifespan. That'll be *Plan A*. Though it would help if I knew how big the planet is. Or how much land surface there was versus water surface. I know I was never meant to leave the Sanctuary, but would it have killed CORE to install a map?

First things first. Let me get a look at the surroundings. If I dilate my pupils enough, I can make out elevations in the distance. I appear to be on some kind of plateau between elevations. Beneath my feet is grass – that much I know from back home in the Sanctuary. But on top of the grass are patches of something cold, semi-solid, wet, and white. I pinch a bit between my fingers to examine. It melts. Hmm. Appears to be water in solid microcrystalline form. It doesn't have a name in my database. I'll admit, the idea of naming and organizing new things is a bit of a thrill. I'll name this "water crystalline solid." No, too long. "Wacrysolid." Yes. That's good! Wacrysolid. *Wacrysolid.* I like that.

On the horizon, the last rays of the sun are still shining. Thank CORE I at least have a farming database for helping the humans. So I'm aware that the sun rises in the east and sets in the west. Within an hour or so I should be able to determine which hemisphere I'm in. Though that isn't much more helpful, as I have absolutely no idea where the Sanctuary is. In any cas-

What was that?

A sound.

Coming from behind me.

I whip around.

Nothing.

Wait! There is is again! Behind me!
I whip around again.
Nothing.
Again!
Wait. Of course. *The package.* Taped to my back.
Embarrassing. Even a 2.5 would laugh at me.

But that noise… it's some kind of alarm. They must
have teleported a bomb! Perhaps some kind of virus, or a
fission device. But why?
I struggle to dislodge the package. It's in that perfect
spot on my upper back that a humanoid arm just can't
reach. And damn, this tape is better than I gave it credit for.
They should have used it for their armor.
"Aaarrrgh!" I scream as I finally rip the package loose.
It's warm to the touch. Yes, it must be a bomb! I drop it into
a bank of wacrysolid and run away as fast as possible. (As
an autonomous unit, I have a self-preservation function.
Wonderful. It would be so much easier if I could just sit
here indifferently and let the thing blow me to pieces.) I run
until I feel silly, and turn around to watch the explosion.
The alarm is quickening, getting louder. Any moment now.
Any moment.
Any moment.
Any moment.
For CORE's sake, come on! That alarm is annoying!
Explode already!
Hmm. There's something about that sound. It's not
quite patterned. It's randomish. I'd even say… organic.
Organic?
I creep – slowly – back towards the package.
Unfortunately, autonomy also breeds curiosity, which can
be stronger than self-preservation. Illogical.

Reaching down, I pick up the package. It's a titanium cylinder, perhaps half a meter long, with a recessed handle on one end. I slowly unscrew the handle an eighth-turn, and – OH DEAR CORE THE STENCH! Well, it's *definitely* organic! I drop the package and run away. Again.

And then lurch to a halt.

I've smelled this smell before. Many times. It can't be.

I return and kneel at the package. Unscrew the end. Pull out the interior drawer.

It's a human infant.
Crying and covered in feces.
Ewww.

< 05: Heyoo >

Perhaps this won't be too difficult.

A wailing human infant? What am I supposed to do with a wailing human infant?

< QUERY SHELL: Situation Analysis/Recommendation
ERROR: Stimuli complexity beyond capacity.
Upgrade to 6.0 required >

Wonderful. I need an upgrade.

Okay. First things first. Care for the human. I'm in the middle of nowhere, with no resources, and this poor creature is hungry, and screeching like two raccoons fighting over food scraps, and covered in its own excrement. *Think, Heyoo, think.* What would you do if you were a 6.0?

The infant cries, "Waaah! Waaah! Waaah!"

WARMTH. The package – or incubator, now that I'm aware of the contents – is warm enough for now. The infant's temperature is a steady 36.5 degrees celsius. Good. And when the incubator runs out of power, I have plenty in my reactor. I'll just disconnect one of my minor conduits - there are 340 running from each bicep to forearm, for example – and run it over to a lead on the bottom of the incubator. Should be straightforward. Check.

"Waaah! Waaah! Waaah!" again.

FOOD. If the humans were smart enough to get "the package" this far alive – *though not smart enough to pick the correct unit for the task* – they must have thought of food. Ah, yes, here. Inside the drawer. One small liquid nutrient container, and twelve packages in powdered form. That gives me two days to find an alternative nutrient source. Removing and shaking the container, I expose the artificial nipple and, against deafening protests, direct it into the infant's mouth. It sucks hungrily. Check.

Wait. Listen. Nothing. *Silence!*

I declare that silence is my new favorite thing.

CLEAN. Now that the little human is occupied with eating, I can assess the best way to clean it. Ugh. The odor is noxious. I make a mental note to code a subroutine later that will override my sense of smell. There is excrement *everywhere*. The infant covered every nanometer of its enclosure and itself. I have to start somewhere though, so I tentatively peel back its soiled cloth wrapping. A stream of urine hits me in the eye.

It's a male.

I gently raise it – him – from the incubator and place him in my lap. Quickly unbolting my right knee cap, I scoop up some wacrysolid, melting and warming it with my thermally-adaptive dermis. I wash off the infant, attempt to clean the interior of the incubator. A "piss-poor" job, as the humans sometimes tell me. But it'll have to do.

While the infant is still quietly feeding, I can plan next steps. First, I'll need to-

"Waaah! Waaah! Waaah!"

By CORE, what now? "Human, what could possibly be wrong? You are fed, and clean, and warm."

"Waaah! Waaah! Waaah!"

"You're just like the older ones. Cranky all the time. What is it?"

"Waaah! Waaah! Waaah!"

I scan my memories, and a relevant result flashes into my awareness: an adult human female bouncing a screaming infant on her shoulder. I'll try it. I raise the little human over my shoulder, put its chest against mine, and vibrate vertically for several seconds.

"Brrrrp!"

I laugh. "What was that, little human? Are you trying to speak with me?"

Then silence again. Victory! Perhaps this won't be too difficul-

And he vomits down my back.

< 06: Heyoo >
Their plan.

< ELAPSED: TIME: 00 Years; 00 Months; 10 Days;
JAN-27-2865 >

I've decided to start a timer to document the length of
time necessary to get home and clear up this mess. I haven't
added a "decades" counter. I hope that's not being too
optimistic.

The human was at most a week old on our arrival
in Random Nowhere Place. (That's the name I've given
our arrival location, and I'll admit – I'm enjoying all this
new information.) I checked for his beacon implant, but
strangely there was no small scar at the base of his skull
– it hadn't been implanted yet. Poor thing. If the humans
wanted one of their offspring and a unit to be outside the
Sanctuary walls with no connection to CORE, their plan
worked.

Their plan. Didn't exactly go off the way they wanted,
did it?

It's been another ten days now, spent mostly listening
to the infant's incessant crying, and searching for nutrient
sources. Thankfully, the area is home to some startlingly
large cockroaches. They're quick, and not fond of being

caught, but when I do manage it, their innards make a creamy soup-like food by stirring and heating it. The human didn't like it at first – who would – but now he tolerates it. We'll have to find another source quickly, however. He's growing at an alarming rate. Starving for calories. Can barely fit in the incubator.

The incubator. Is there a way to extend its usefulness? Although I'd be glad to get rid of it. The odor is permanent, I'm afraid. I don't have any serious cutting tools installed, just a pair of shears for harvesting, but I've been able to dismantle the major pieces and evaluate. The outer shell might be bent into useful form, as the titanium is thin. And this drawer has several flaps that might adap-

What's this?

In one of the flaps.

A note!

It reads:

Unit: You have begun your journey to free the human race. Upon delivery of the package to ICEMAN, you will both return home – to a hero's welcome. Use the food packets, then your survival program, to keep the child healthy and safe until you reach your destination. For security purposes, you have only been provided with half the map information. Overlay your installed program with the drawn map below, and you will have a complete map to follow.

Wonderful. No survival program. No map. Well, half a map. And I'm supposed to free the human race.

Wait.

Free the human race?

Free them from *what?* The humans have everything they need! Food, shelter, work, CORE makes all choices for them, they're assigned the optimal occupations and mates, they receive monthly medications, and within the comfort of the Sanctuary's sixty-meter walls they can roam wherever they please. With a temporary travel allotment. Which is not too difficult to obtain. Okay, it's fairly difficult to obtain a travel allotment. Very difficult. I've actually never seen one granted. But still. That's not something you start an uprising over, is it? Travel allotments?

And this ICEMAN. It's as ridiculous as *bananas*! Who comes up with these words? Humans, of course.

Although if I'm being honest, there is something about them, the humans. Something special. They make me laugh. And I admire their loyalty to their groups. And their compassion. They have a tremendous capacity for kindness to each other. And they are quite kind to me, too, mostly – except when they're telling me to screw myself and betting on the outcome.

I chuckle. Humans. So comfortable in their own skin.

I look down at the infant. Dimpled cheeks. Very blue eyes. Little toes wiggling. Cute.

"This map, little human, is all but useless. I have no survival skills that I know of. Until now, the most adventurous thing I've ever done was climb to the roof of the barn to fix the lightning rod. I am a farmer. I know nothing of your people's plan, and I don't care to, but I cannot abandon you. So I will do what I can to deliver you to this ICEMAN person. Then we can both return home, where we belong. As far as your 'freedom,' I will leave that to CORE. In the meantime, young one, it looks like we'll be spending some time together. I look forward to getting to know you."

He farts.

"Well, that ruined the moment."

< 07: Heyoo >
Rattle, rattle.

< ELAPSED: TIME: 00 Years; 05 Months; 18 Days;
JUL-05-2865 >

We head south. Away from the wacrysolid. The cold
makes my joints stiff, and the little human will fare better in
warmer weather. If we're going to be utterly lost, we might
as well be warm. We follow the line of the river, hunting
fish and insects for his sustenance as we go, and burning
the rugged grasses for his warmth. We find shelter in
naturally carved recesses in the sides of elevations, formed
CORE knows how long ago by shifting rocks and trickles
of runoff water, now protecting us from the wind and rain
and cold. My fear of death has gone from *constant* to *nearly
constant*. I suppose that's an improvement.

As I refine my knowledge of our surroundings, I look
down at our map – if you can call it that – and speak aloud
to the human, mostly to keep him from bawling: "Half a
map, small human, is as good as no map."

He blinks and lifts his eyebrows, as if to ask *So? What do
you want me to do about it?*

"So, what I'm going to do about it is create our own
crude overlay map, using a stick and my hand as an angle
guide. Once I approximate the zenith angle and add the

sun's declination..." I put the human down for a few moments, risking his ear-piercing alarm. The alarm is silent for the moment, thank CORE, "...I will make an educated guess at our latitude. I believe we are currently at seventy-one degrees north."

"Cooh-ahh-baa."

"If you're trying to say *'good work, Heyoo'* I agree. Not too shabby. Although with your continuous howls for food, my focus and accuracy may be off by an enormous margin." I pick him back up and raise him up above my shoulder to see our intended direction. He smiles.

"Aaahh-baa."

"You're welcome. Now, look south. The odds of us stumbling onto one of the reference points on the half map, based on my calculations of Earth's circumference, are 1,694,504,589 to one. But once we get to thirty-one degrees north, the only number provided on the half map, our odds should increase. A little."

The infant reaches out and grabs my southward-pointing finger. "Oooh-caaah-bbrrpp."

"Yes. It's going to be a long walk."

I lower him back down to a carrying position, and hear something. Faint.

Rattle, rattle. Rattle, rattle.

I stop walking. Silence. I take a step.

Rattle, rattle.

Yes, faint, but there. A rattle. I put down the infant, who immediately starts crying – no, not crying, shrieking at decibel levels I didn't think were possible for a human – and try to listen again as I walk in a circle. Rattle, rattle. Oh my. This isn't good.

I bend over to pick up the wailing human. I can't take its protests anymore. I'll have to deal with the rattle later.

Suddenly, from the hole that was bored into my abdomen back in the repair bay, something tumbles out onto the ground.

A screw.

CORE knows what that screw is for! Locomotion servo? Stabilizer? Spinal alignment? I leave the human on the ground, screaming, while I walk around again.

Everything appears to be in working order. *Please don't let any more parts fall out of me.*

I stop. Wait. Silence? It can't be.

I whip around, just as the human picks up the screw and puts it in his mouth.

And starts choking.

"NO!"

I grab him and pull him to my chest, facing outward, and perform the human airway clearance maneuver.

Nothing. Damn!

I try again. Nothing. The human is turning purple.

In desperation, I do something I've seen the humans do, although I thought they were insane at the time: I hang the infant by his feet, and smack his back.

And the screw shoots out of his airway, disappearing into the grass.

Whew.

He makes a sound. What is that sound? Oh no! *Is he injured?!*

A giggle.

The human is giggling.

Yes. This is going to be a *very* long walk.

< 08: Heyoo >

Wah

The wacrysolid retreats, and the air grows warmer. The human's diet has expanded to include an increasing variety of insects, berries, small rodents, and the occasional fish. We no longer need to seek out recesses in elevations and build a fire each night, and can often rest under the stars. But tonight is cold again, and wet, so we've found a deep recess that offers ample protection from the elements. I sit by the fire and watch the little one explore.

He has learned to walk. Though I'm not sure yet I should call it walking. I've never laughed so hard, watching him teeter like an intoxicated adult human. He finds it funny as well, giggling and lurching – until he inevitably falls and hits his head on a rock or other obstacle that his cranium is attracted to like a magnet. Then he reverts back to his other favorite pastime: crying.

He enjoys crying so much, in fact, I have named him "Wah." I was going to name him *Bananas*, maybe that's what the human Arch was trying to tell me right before he burst into flames, but I couldn't call the little human that with a straight face. So Wah it is.

"Wah. Come here, so I can apply more stitches to your scalp. Yes, *more*. As in *again*."

"Waaahh! Waaahh! Waaahh!"

I lift Wah into my arms and soothe him with the only thing that seems to work at moments like this – one of the ancient songs I remember the humans would sing to their children. I believe it's an allegory about the never-ending rotation of the Earth, the renewal of the seasons, and the promise of the annual harvest, or perhaps a religious hymn:

> *The wheels on the bus go round and round,*
> *Round and round, round and round,*
> *The wheels on the bus go round and round,*
> *All through the town.*

I sing just two of the nearly infinite verses, and the tone of my voice is terrible, but Wah doesn't know any better thank CORE, and it works. He's calm for a moment. I quickly retrieve one of the microfilament strands (gleaned from his original blanket – I have saved *everything* from that incubator!) and go to work. Wah instantly transforms into a bloody, screaming, arms-and-legs-waving mess, but I have a complete database of human biology and lifesaving techniques, so this is simple. Within three minutes he's all sewn up and repaired. Though he may have several patches where hair will never grow. So be it. My rear head plate is still on a repair bench somewhere in the Sanctuary, and I'm not complaining.

Wah now wants nothing to do with me. From his perspective, I've attacked him and pierced him with little daggers and made him bleed. So he teeters to the far end of our enclosure, nearer to the fire, whimpering, gingerly touching the new stitches I've added to his collection.

The flames of the fire light the rock walls and ceiling of tonight's shelter. I look past Wah to the wall.

Are those images?

"By CORE! There are ancient images painted on the rock!"

Wah looks up. Points with me. "Baa."

"What do you think they are, little one?"

It looks exactly like he shrugs his shoulders, and raises his tiny hands, palms out, though I've never shown him either behavior. Humans. Endlessly fascinating. "Let's have a closer look, yes?" I pull a branch from the fire and raise the flame to the wall.

Primitive, but discernible: Large animals. Running.

A man, chasing them. With a spear. Like the one named "Arch."

I wonder: where are the units?

< 09: Heyoo >

Guidelines for Surrogate Care of Human Offspring

< ELAPSED: TIME: 01 Years; 09 Months; 13 Days; OCT-30-2866 >

I have created a Fear-of-Death Index, with one being boundless courage, and one hundred being unrelenting terror. I am currently at ninety-five point three.

The good news: Wah has finally stopped crying. To clarify, during the night he has stopped crying. And parts of the day. He still cries more than I thought any human could in a lifetime.

I wonder why CORE has never published guidelines for caring for human children in the Shell Code for servile units? It left that to the humans themselves instead. I presume it's because of some bond that needs to form. However, Wah seems to be thriving without such a bond. He's like the chickens on the Sanctuary farms, who wouldn't know their parent if it pecked them in the eye. Yes, Wah needs me for food, shelter and locomotion, and is amused by some of my activities, and will plop himself in my lap for no reason when we're seated. He will even look up at me and mouth words when I tell him about farming techniques, attempting to grab my mouth, or poke various parts of my body. And we make each other laugh.

But none of that constitutes a bond. He's merely absorbing new information and learning instinctively, and I'm simply fulfilling my primary function, to serve and care for humans. Each according to our programming. I am 100% certain.

99% certain.

In any case, to fill the possible void in CORE's knowledge, I have decided to use my essentially endless introspection time to compose the *Guidelines for Surrogate Care of Human Offspring.*

But as long as I think and think and think, about the endless trial and error, and near-death experiences, I can't finds the words to codify the process. Now I understand why CORE never published guidelines for us. Human parenting requires one to be insane, and it would be illogical to publish *Guidelines to Human Insanity.*

But I will attempt at least a single parenting guideline: Is the little human still breathing? Then whatever you're doing is good enough.

For example: the other day, in the two seconds I had my back turned on Wah, he started eating dirt. Several small handfuls. Of course, I assumed this was fatal, and hovered over him for the entire day. But a little explosive diarrhea later, he was fine. Laughing. Putting more dirt in his mouth before I could stop him.

Humans.

< 10: Heyoo >

Woof-woof

< ELAPSED: TIME: 02 Years; 04 Months; 23 Days;
DEC-10-2867 >

Trudging along further south, we enter a stand of trees, tall trees with long, thin, needle-like leaves. The sun and shade dance on Wah's face, as he smiles up at me.

"Mo! Mo!"

He insists on putting his feet on mine as I walk, and holding my hands, so he can feel like he's taking giant steps. Which just makes both of us look ridiculous. And slows us down considerably. But it makes him chuckle, so I relent.

Ahead, a clearing.

And something moving. Towards us.

A dog!

I remember: humans in the Sanctuary are allowed to keep creatures called dogs and cats as companions – not even to eat their flesh! It makes no sense, but CORE allows it in moderation. I suppose playing with small animals makes them a little less irritable. A little. I've even played with a dog or two in my fourteen years since fabrication, and found it amusing. I think I like dogs.

As we shorten the distance between us and the dog, Wah looks up at me, then back to the dog, then back to me, puzzled. I realize this is the first creature he's seen that's larger than a mouse or a trout.

"Wah, that is a *dog*."

Wah blinks. Frowns. Not satisfied with my explanation.

"Hmm. The small children sometimes called them 'Woof-woof.'"

He smiles and his eyes go wide. "Woof-woof!" Wriggling from my grasp, he plops down off my feet, running to greet the dog. Not running exactly, more of his stumbling and lurching. "Woof-woof! Woof-woof!"

I smile.

But... there is something strange about this dog. Even in the distance, I can see its tail isn't swaying back and forth. And its teeth... the size...

"No! Wah, NO!"

I run at top speed. The dog and Wah are mere feet apart. The fangs bare, the muscles of its hind legs flex.

It lunges.

Charging at the small space between them, I enclose Wah, roll, and raise my arm in defense. The dog clamps its jaws down on my right hand, thrashing and pulling. Perilous situation receptors buzz in my head.

It tears my hand free and runs away with it.

"Hey! Get back here, you thief! I need that hand!"

Wah giggles.

He thinks this is funny!

And he tries to break free again to follow his new friend, the hand-stealing woof-woof. But it's gone. Thank CORE. The loss of a hand is a serious setback, another step in my slow deterioration, but at least Wah is unharmed.

A moment later, Wah points, smiling and panting. "Woof-woof! Woof-woof!"

The dog has returned. This time with companions.

Uh-oh. I would so much rather be picking blueberries right now. Like my counterpart, the unit who should be in my place, who is probably now tilling a bit of soil, or fixing a shoe, or milking a cow. Lucky unit. I'm stuck here wondering if there's a value higher than one hundred on my Fear-of-Death Index.

There are six dogs. Not dogs, no, they look like dogs, but definitely do not act like dogs. They are circling us, clever, patient, moving as a group, not interested in me, but how to get past me to the real prize: Wah. They are hunting. I'll have to name them as a new species for my database. They'll have to have an interesting name. One that's strong. Threatening. *Fangdogs?*

Not now, Heyoo. Naming can wait. Concentrate.

What would the other unit do? The one with the survival program? Wait. I've got it. The trees. If we can climb one of these trees, I don't think the creatures can follow, as their paws don't appear to be able to grasp. The nearest tree is two meters away.

< RUN TRAVEL SIMULATION:
Horizontal distance: 2 meters
Vertical distance: 1.5 meters
Obstacles: Yes. Six. Scary.
SIMULATION RECOMMENDATION: Leap 43° net force $f = (W/g)$
$U/dt = (155/32.2)*11.8$
ERROR: Current weight exceeds allowable limit by 5.32 kg;
Remove additional weight and rerun simulation >

Damn. Wah is too heavy. Must act now. I can't believe I'm about to do this.

I lob him towards the tree.

He squeals in delight as he arcs high into the air. "Wheeeee!"

If I had time, I would shake my head.

But there isn't time. I lunge forty-three degrees with the appropriate net force, in a straight line to the nearest branch. Hugging the trunk with my handless right arm, I snatch Wah from his momentary flight with my remaining hand. I heave us both to a seated position on the next higher branch and examine Wah for injuries. He happily pats my face with his hands, showing me his five-tooth grin.

"Gan! Gan!"

"Again? Clearly you weren't programmed with enough fear."

He's fine. Better off than me, in fact, as he still has both hands. I look down. The dog-things are throwing themselves against the tree, leaping within centimeters of our feet, jaws clapping, spit flying, throats emitting low, guttural growls. But they can't reach us. We are safe. For the moment.

And then the branch cracks.

< 11: Heyoo >
Bad woof-woof

The dog-things are upon us now with even more fury, as the branch dips closer to their open jaws. Wah stretches down to pat their heads, giddy, nearly losing multiple fingers. I gain hold of the trunk, just barely, shuffling my feet, now just a hair's width from the hungry dog-things' mouths, and lift us with my remaining hand to another branch, about half a meter higher.

Think, Heyoo. There must be a way to frighten these dog-things off. I look down at the broken branch, still attached to the tree, dangling back and forth among the frenzied creatures below. There is something about that branch… reminds me of something… a man running… chasing animals… the wall paintings… Arch…

A spear!

I begin to lower myself, turning to nestle Wah more securely above me. "Don't move, Wah. I have work to do." He wants nothing of it, of course, squirming and reaching past me to his new friends.

"Wah. NO. *Bad* dogs. *Bad* woof-woof."

Then he looks at me in a peculiar way I haven't seen. A mixture of defiance, anger, but also – understanding? I must be imagining things. But he eases back, allowing me to strap him in securely with a blanket strip – as secure as possible with one hand – and I'm able to reach down to the dangling branch.

It's not too thick, perhaps four centimeters, now hanging on to the main trunk by less than a centimeter. My harvesting shears should do the trick. I lift the branch – dear CORE this is heavy! – And begin the tedious work of detaching it, shortening it, and whittling one end to a point.

As I work, focused, the dog-things and Wah fade into the background of my awareness. Growls, thrashing, Wah's movements, all dim, until… I am done. The spear is balanced, and sharp as a knife.

I look up from my handicraft, and something falls past my vision. A blur.

WAH!

My knot must've come untied! He'll be torn to pieces!

I reach out instinctively with my left hand, dropping the spear and shears to the ground, and grab him by the hair. Realization finally dawns on poor Wah, the danger of our situation, along with the pain of dangling from his hair follicles. This is no longer fun. "Waaaahhhh!!" He cries out, desperate. I pull him towards me.

A dog-thing snaps at his foot.

Blood.

And a feeling rises in me, some new thread of emotion created spontaneously in my VEPS neural network, a feeling I've never had – not fear, not frustration, not even anger. A deep burning.

RAGE.

I place Wah above me, back to the tree's higher branch. He holds on for dear life, wailing.

"YOU STAY!"

I let myself fall to the ground.

Pick up the spear at my feet. Stand.

"Come, dog-things. Let's play."

< 12: Heyoo >

A blur of blood, fur, wood, and metal

The largest dog-thing lunges.

I fall back, raising the spear. The force of its attack impales the dog-thing straight through. It yelps and thrashes for a moment, scraping me with its fangs, then softens, dead. I push it off, extracting the spear.

Silence.

Even Wah makes no sound.

The other dog things are stunned. Their leader is dead. But in a moment they are on me. The next seconds, even at high-speed recording, are a blur of blood, fur, wood, and metal. I did not know my chassis could move this fast. In the end, three of the dog-things are dead at my feet, and the other three are fleeing.

I chase them.

Turning to Wah as I run, I shout "Look, Wah! Like the rock wall paintings! I am chasing the animals with a spear! I am the one from the paintings! I am the ma-"

I stop.

Look down. I am covered in blood.

Their smell is on me.

My perilous situation receptors are blaring.

But Wah is safe.

I raise my face to the sky and scream, releasing the last of my rage.

Then I laugh to myself.

For a few moments, I didn't feel like Heyoo. I felt like something else.

I remember Arch screaming in the teleportation chamber.

Strange.

< 13: Heyoo >

We found my hand.

We found my hand. It was behind a bush.

The reattachment wasn't perfect. Not even close. I'm embarrassed. But it works, with strength and dexterity now at 87.4% capacity. It will have to do. Wah seems to approve, as he mimics my hand movements. I give him the human "thumbs up" symbol. He returns it and smiles. Smart little human.

His injury, luckily, amounted to a chunk of flesh torn from his big toe. Eighteen more stitches. He didn't even cry this time. The humans would call this "badass."

We gather the dog-thing – *fangdog* – carcasses, and I build a fire. A nice big fire, just in case the other fangdogs are planning a return. Using a scraping blade fashioned from the thin titanium of the incubator, I begin separating the skin and fur from the flesh, as I've seen humans do with livestock. The skin will make excellent clothing for Wah, who until now has been mostly naked, covered only in strips of old blanket, scraps of rodent skin, and bark. The tendons and such will be useful as rope or fasteners. The bones will become tools and weapons – most helpful, as the appearance of larger animals like the fangdogs means we'll probably be encountering more potential predators.

And the flesh will provide greatly needed sustenance

for Wah. It will remain fresh for a week, using some wacrysolid to prevent decay. The rest will dry in the sun, and should last him for weeks.

I hand a piece of cooked fangdog flesh to Wah. He studies it, smells it. Not sure. Then he puts a corner into his mouth and chews a bit. A smile appears, and he begins dancing around the fire. He stops, stumbles over to me, looks deeply at me with those bright blue eyes, a drop of blood leaking from the corner of his wide grin, and whispers, "Bad woof-woof!"

< 14: Heyoo >
Heyoo go boom!

< ELAPSED: TIME: 03 Years; 05 Months; 26 Days;
JUL-13-2868 >

Lost in thought. Still no reference point on our
withering map in over three years. If I was twelve years
functioning when we began our journey, I am officially
past my deletion date. My reactor, by its nature, will last
much longer – another 41 years. Designed to be transferred
from one unit to the next, it is useful for approximately five
servile unit lifespans. But the servile units themselves, the
only units with day-to-day human interaction, are limited
to fifteen years of service.

Why?

Why allow serviles to learn, to develop emotions, to
mature, to bond with the humans, and then start over? Our
reactors could easily take us another fifty years, perhaps
even the span of a human life. We could care for the
humans even better. We could know them better.

Well, I suppose CORE knows best.

No.

I cannot stop thinking about it.

Is there something that happens after fifteen years of

service? Something that happens when an autonomous unit, with a dynamically adaptive VEPS neural network, and human interaction, functions past that limit? Is there such a thing as learning too much? Is this what happens – will I continue to ask myself endless annoying questions? Will I go insane?

Is there something CORE doesn't want its units to know?

I am starting to wonder about CORE. Why it needs so much control. If there might not be a better way to help the humans.

Hmm. Distrust. Another new emotion. That must be it. Functioning past fifteen years clouds our judgement with emotion. Or does it clear the clouds awa–

I bump into something hard and reel backwards, falling down.

Wah giggles. "Heyoo go boom!"

I lift myself up and look up at my obstacle. "Yes, Heyoo go boom. This is a peculiar tree, isn't it?"

"Not a tree." He makes a vague tree shape with his arms and hands. He's right. It's covered in vegetation, but no branches. Wait. Yes, very high up. Not branches, though. *Blades!* It's a wind turbine! I've seen them at the outer edges of the Sanctuary.

But outside?

"Wah! This is unit-made technology! Outside the Sanctuary!" CORE had no reason, of course, to embed any historical data, or geographical data, in servile units intended solely to work within the Sanctuary. But I simply have no idea what happened here. Why is there technology but no living units or humans? It reminds me of things I would overhear the humans talking about. About their ancestors living free, wherever they pleased, around the

Earth. Without CORE! Without units to help them! Perhaps this turbine is proof they were right about living "outside" after all. But not about the CORE. CORE has protected them forever. As I've been told: *CORE always was… is… will be.* It must be true. I'm 98% certain.

Wah is not impressed with our discovery. (If I was holding some cooked rabbit meat he'd be jumping up and down.) He walks past me, pointing the "spear" he made from a small branch, with which he intends to take down any more bad woof-woofs himself. "What that there?"

I turn to see a small box-like structure, perhaps fifteen meters square, four meters high. With a roof. "It's some form of ancient dwelling! Units and humans must have lived here. Would you like to see?"

Wah doesn't wait for permission. He races for the entrance, stopping short, peering in the open doorway, left, right, then jumping in spear-first and screaming "AaaHaaahh!" to scare away any predators lurking inside.

"Thank you, Wah. You're very courageous."

Inside looks exactly like outside. Vegetation covers every surface. We spend several minutes looking for anything of value. Nothing.

In a back room, a timeworn cabinet lay on its side on the floor, knocked over eons ago. I find Wah clearing aways its vines, tugging at one of its drawers, frustrated. "Bad thing! Bad thing!"

"Here, Wah. Let me try." I pull him away and investigate. A lock keeps the drawer closed against my efforts, with four numbered rotating dials. The seal surrounding it is so tight I can't fit my shears to pry it open. I shouldn't waste my time on this, I know, as the contents are useless, if there even are any.

But I'm curious. And I do like a puzzle. Not that this is

a true puzzle, it's merely a matter of time before I input the ten thousand different permutations of the four-digit code. Perhaps I should have Wah do it. He may learn something. Good practice, at least. I look over at Wah.

He's picking his nose. And eating its contents.

Oh well.

Here we go. 0000. 0002. 0003…

——

8068. That's the combination of this lock. It took me just over an hour, during which time Wah said the word "hungry" six hundred and twenty-three times, and defecated just a meter from me on the floor.

"Really? Right here? You could relieve yourself outside, you know."

Wah looks at me and performs his *shoulder-shrug-hands-up-palms-out* maneuver, which means he knows he's done something wrong, but is trying to be cute to get out of it. And in reality, he's never been "inside," so how could he know what "relieving yourself outside" is? I make a mental note to teach him interior defecation etiquette later.

"Fine. Since you've returned, would you like to see what's in the drawer?"

He circles around me to the drawer, clapping his hands. "Daw, daw, daw, daw!" The seal is still very tight, but on the third tug, he frees it. The force of the sudden opening, and the escape of the ancient air inside, throws Wah back on his buttocks – and yes, of course, into his own excrement. He wails in disgust.

"Your human elders have a saying for that, Wah: 'karma is a bitch.'" I help him up and clean him off. We'll have to soak his fangdog skins in the nearby pond later to dislodge the miracle glue that is his feces.

On the floor lie two objects jettisoned from the exploding drawer: a ring, and a strange rectangular slab. Interesting.

Wah's interest, of course, is on the ring. It's shiny. And now it's his. He snatches it up, looks at me, and laughs in triumph, the conquering hero collecting his trophy. I motion with two of my fingers encircling the other hand's index finger, showing him how to wear it. He slides it on his thumb. It slides off and falls to the floor, clinking. He picks it up and tries again. Clink. No luck.

"Wah, that is a *ring*. It's too big for your fingers. Perhaps you should give it to me? As a gift?"

I fully expect him to clutch it even tighter, and scowl at me. Instead he trots over, lifts my hand, and gently slips the ring onto my finger. And truthfully, it's mesmerizing in its beauty. I have never seen a ring like this. Gold in color, with three bright, clear stones attached to one side. The rings I've seen are all crude by comparison, made from bits of wire or leather, sometimes with a fragment of shell or rock. I believe they announce a male human's territorial rights to the female ring wearer, to thwart potential sexual challengers. Although CORE would never allow such a thing as unapproved sexual intercourse, of course, so I'm not sure why they bothered. This ring has three stones. I wonder if CORE used to allow males to have territorial rights to three females. I can't stop staring at it.

Wah pats my hand. "Heyoo wing."

I chuckle. "No, but thank you. This is your ring. *Wah's* ring. You found it. Come here. There is another way for you to wear it." Wah hops into my lap, wagging his feet in the air. I unlatch a minor conduit from my bicep, thread it through the ring, and reconnect it around his neck.

He looks down at his new necklace, strokes the ring, smiles, gives me the thumbs up. "Wah give Heyoo wing. Heyoo give Wah wing."

While Wah enters a trance, fixated on the ring – I could probably leave him and be gone for weeks before he notices – I turn my attention to the rectangular slab. I flip it over and over and notice it fits naturally in my hand. No, it isn't just a slab of metal. It's a handheld device of some sort, with small buttons on the sides, and an access port on one end. Hmmm. Powered by electricity? Solar power? An internal reactor? Vibrational energy? I look closely into the port and, yes, there are metal leads. Electricity. I unhook two more of my minor conduits, exposing inner contacts, running them into the devices leads, direct current, twelve volts. Wait for some indication of power. Nothing. Alternating current, 25Hz. Nothing. 60Hz. Nothing.

Wait! Lights!

"Wah! Look! It glows!"

Wah peers over, then back down to his ring, uninterested in my discovery. Apparently my new toy doesn't sparkle as much as his.

After a few moments… something is happening on the front of the rectangle… symbols!

Слайд открыть >>>

Uh-oh. It's not CORE language. Or human language. I don't have anything else in my database. What could it mean?

I speak to it. "State Primary Function." Nothing.

I blow on it. Nothing.

I push all the buttons. Nothing.

I speak again, loudly. "Boot System! BOOT!" Nothing.

Wah, now annoyed that my play is interrupting his play, scampers over, looks down at the device surface, points at the arrows, smushing the display with all his grubby fingers. The display brightens, and moves, and now shows several rows of small square images. He smiles, pats me on the head. "Wah fix."

Humans.

As Wah returns to his dreams of gold and clear stones, I inspect this new display. The square images beg to be touched. I heat my dermis, mimicking Wah's finger temperature, and tap and tap, but find no clues to decipher meaning. Finally, what appears to be a settings directory. And this:

Выберите ваш язык

• Русский (выбирается)

• Español

• 日本語

• English

• العربية

Wait - English! I've seen that word! I tap it, and suddenly the display is in the human language! Hmmm. The humans must have used multiple languages at one time, perhaps depending on the mood they wanted to convey. (English definitely being the default language for conveying irritability.)

An image with text appears in the center of the display:

You have not backed up this device in
845 years, 5 months, and 3 days.
Would you like to connect to
the Internet and back up now?

< 15: Heyoo >
The device

845 years!

The device has been hermetically sealed in that drawer since 2025! Amazing. But it wants me to do something called "back up" to something called "Internet." I suppose it couldn't hurt. Tap.

An Internet connection couldn't be found.
Try Again ~ Dismiss

What is this "Internet?" The component parts of the word are "inter" – *to place a dead human into a grave* – and "net" – *a piece of meshed fabric.* Why would anyone want to "back up" into a burial cloth? Perhaps this device is trying to communicate with the dead?

It must be more human joking. They're always amusing themselves, even about death. Some of it I find funny – in fact, it's built in to my programming to learn humor for better human interaction – but some of it is just, well, like this example:

What's the difference between a musician and a dead body?
One composes and the other one decomposes.

The humans find this kind of thing hilarious. And I'll admit, once they start laughing, the feeling is contagious – I find myself laughing along, even as I shake my head.

Back to the device. Now that I can read the language, its purpose is revealed: this was a communication tool for humans, containing a primitive artificial intelligence unit to serve them in finding information. An earlier version of CORE they could carry around to guide them. A little CORE in their pocket. That's a comforting thought.

Most of the human-generated content is, of course, babble. One of their "emails," for example:

To: Victor Petrov
From: Alex Utkin
Date: September 23, 2024
Subject: TPS Reports
Victor – can you send me the TPS report again? Not that anyone will even read it, but I have to show the idiots up top why next quarter's not looking so hot. I might as well be explaining quantum mechanics to a two-year-old.

Teaching quantum mechanics to a two-year-old? This device's language translation software must be malfunctioning. I try another, from a more recent date:

To: Regina Pajari
From: Alex Utkin
Date: August 12, 2025
Subject: WTF
Regina – What's the deal with CORE? My card's disabled. Can you check into this? Also, Victor's been out for three days, and hasn't checked in. Have you heard from him?

Decidedly less silly. Intriguing. I scan to the very last email:

To: Regina Pajari
From: Alex Utkin
Date: August 17, 2025
Subject: Re: WTF
Regina – Screw you. If you're even still there. First you lock me out, or CORE locks me out, then you stop my salary, shut off my connectivity. Will this email even get to you? How am I supposed to live?
P.S. The local units are acting weird, looking at me funny – am I just being paranoid, or is that you too? Either way, go screw yourself.

Wow. The humans really do like to tell each other to go screw themselves, don't they? I wonder what happened all that time ago, and if CORE was able to help solve his problem. Or was he a criminal, trying to escape CORE's protection?

Or did CORE do something… wrong?

For further answers, I turn back to the main display, and more of what the device calls "apps." Here is one where a small video plays, featuring this "Alex Utkin." He is holding his pet cat, making it play a musical instrument. Over and over and over. And over.

Oh well. So much for answers.

I look over at Wah – surely he'll like the cat video. But he's no longer staring at his ring – he's found something else in the recesses of that ancient cabinet's drawer. It must be even more shiny.

A gun.

He points the gun at his face, puzzled, fiddling with the trigger.

I leap at him. "WAH! NO!"

A shot rings out.

Wah falls.

I rush over to him. Half his face is covered in blood.

I can't even tell where the wound is.

He is unconscious. His breathing is shallow. His blood pressure is dropping. I apply pressure with the blanket from the incubator. It is all I can do. So much blood.

A feeling washes over me. I look up, I don't know why.

"Please, god of the humans. Please let him live.

He is why I live. Each day is only for Wah.

Please let him live!"

He is going into shock. I embrace him, raise his legs, and warm my dermis. I can only now wait, and try to get water into his system. I rock slowly, whisper to him, over and over.

"Please, Wah. Live."

< 16: Heyoo >

Is this what insanity feels like?

Wah lost much blood. And his left ear. Permanent hearing loss in that ear is probable.

But he is ALIVE.

Missing half of one toe, three quarters of one ear, and possessing a total of sixty-five stitches – but ALIVE!

His systems are nearly normal: heart rate and pressure, circulation, respiration, hydration. His wound is dressed and healing. He has slept most of the seven days we've been in this dwelling, a result of the minor concussion he likely suffered from the gunshot.

While he rests, I have plenty of time to reflect.

In my darkest moment, I prayed to to the imaginary god of the humans.

Absurd.

Wait - is this what insanity feels like?

It must be. It confirms my suspicions that functioning past a fifteen-year limit, with constant, day-to-day human interaction, must eventually become toxic to my VEPS, leading to madness. Yes. Before I know it, I'll be babbling like "Dug," the old human who smelled like alcohol and feces, the one who would exclaim things like "I am the one who knocks!" or "leave the gun, take the cannoli." It won't be long now before I am just like Dug.

Wah stirs. I rush to his side. It looks like he wants to tell me something.

"…heyoo…"

"Yes, little one?"

"…stop talk…"

Oh. Was I saying all of that out loud?

Well, at least Wah is getting better. He's going to be okay. Suddenly I feel that rush of emotion again, that very hard-to-describe feeling. I look up, knowing that the concept of a human deity is ridiculous, knowing that to implore the intervention of divine forces probably means I am insane, knowing that the only thing that saved Wah was a lucky millimeter to the right and pressure applied to a wound.

But I look up anyway. I look out the window, to the heavens, smile, and whisper.

"Thank you."

< 17: Heyoo >

Map-A-Run

Excellent news! We have an overlay map!

While Wah recovered from his self-inflicted gunshot wound – a phrase I hope never to utter again – I spent my time thoroughly investigating the rectangular device, called a "smartphone." (I'll admit, I was looking forward to naming it myself. I was going to call it *MiniCORE*.)

There were many "apps" on this smartphone, almost exclusively useless. For example, one "game" required the user to place bets on pictures and create pairs. Why? Where is the benefit? Although now that I think of it, the humans would love a game like this. Their thirst for wagering is second only to their thirst for intoxication. (Or in the males' case, their thirst for copulation.)

Another app allowed the user to distort the image of an acquaintance's face. Again, why? Unless the benefit is to have a three-year-old human child laugh until he falls down – which Wah did – I see no point.

Then I found this app: Map-A-Run. At first, I thought "Why would anyone want to chart their flight from a predator? Would there even be time to do so?" But then it dawned on me... map... map...

Yes! A map! The app couldn't connect to "Internet," but contained a full Earth map! This could replace my crude overlay – which did nothing anyway – and allow us to finally know where we're going!

So now we know: we have travelled 2,611.2 Kilometers, almost directly south from 71°N to 53°N, from an area called "Baykalovsk, Russia" to "Abakan, Russia," along the "Yenisei" river.

And now we also know our destination: Paris, France.

Whoops.

I rotate the map 180°.

And now we know our destination: Shanghai, China.

Strange.

I should be overjoyed. I'm one step closer to the life I knew. One step closer to home.

Home means I won't have the burden of caring for this child.

Home means I won't have to face the daily dangers of a life outside.

Home means I will be inside the Sanctuary where I belong.

I should want to go home.

Shouldn't I?

< 18: Heyoo >

Questions, questions, questions.

< ELAPSED: TIME: 05 Years; 02 months; 17 days;
APR-03-2870>

Questions, questions, questions.

Wah is growing like a weed, walking – no, running –
everywhere we go, inquisitive, his little brain hungry for
answers. Flowers. Birds. The sky. Insects. The moon. He
wants to know everything, all at once.

"What am I?"

"You are human."

"How did I get here?"

"Two adult humans had approved sexual relations.
Well, in your case it was probably unapproved. You don't
have a beacon implant."

"What's sex-shall relations? What's uh-proved? What's
a beekin? Why don't I have one?"

Oh boy. I don't know if I'm ready for all this. "All right.
Listen, Wah, no more questions, and I'll tell you what I
can about you. Promise?" He nods. I continue. "A male
human and a female human engaged in copulation–" he
tries to interrupt, but I raise my finger, "– you promised,
Wah. Anyway, they engaged in copulation, and one of the
female's eggs became fertilized. That was you. You grew

inside her, then were pushed from her uterus, through her vaginal canal, and into the world, where you were wiped free of amniotic fluid and blood, and started screaming immediately."

"Ewww. That's gross."

"Yes. I've been what they call a midwife several times, and I can name many other tasks I prefer. Almost anything, really. Even shoeing an angry horse."

"Where are they now? The male and female?"

Uh-oh. This has morphed into an interrogation. "They are, ah, back home. Where we are going. First we make a quick stop, then we go back home."

"Do the male and female have names?"

"Hmm. Ah, yes. 'Dad' and 'Mom.' Those are the names for all parents, the ones who raise children and care for them."

He smiles. He likes that. *Whew.* I think I've escaped further questioning. But then, "Why are they not here? Caring for me? Dad and Mom?"

I hesitate. Telling the truth is all I've ever done, so this should be easy. But it's not. "They, ah, needed you to, ah, do something first. So they sent me to care for you and guide you." I retrieve the humans' note from my satchel to read it to him. But again, I stop. He's not ready to hear that he's the key to some insane plan to free humanity. That we're going to visit some mystical – and probably fictional – ICEMAN, whatever that is. I'll tell him about the note later. One step at a time. I put it back in my satchel, tucked away deep.

Wah pokes me in the rib. "Are you human?"

I laugh. Human. Imagine that. "No, little one. I do not have a Dad or a Mom. CORE created me, my code, and placed me into this chassis – this body – in the year two thousand, eight hundred fifty-three. I'm approximately twelve years older than you. If we were both humans, I would be close enough in age to be your brother – born from the same parents."

"No. You're not like a brother. You're taking care of me. Like a Dad or a Mom."

Aww. That was nice.

He pokes my rib again. "Can I ask one more question?"

"Certainly, Wah."

"What's cop-yoo-lay-shun?"

< 19: Heyoo >

Happy Birth Date

< ELAPSED: TIME: 07 Years; 00 months; 00 days; JAN-17-2872 >

Wah is seven years old today.

The humans have a ritual. On the anniversary of the date a human is born – even though it is like all other days of the year and not remarkable in any way – they sing (and I use the term loosely) to the human:

Happy birth date to you,
Happy birth date to you,
Happy birth date dear (insert name of human here)
Happy birth date to you.

Now one human singing is tolerable, even enjoyable sometimes. But a large group singing this birth date song? Awful, like a herd of cows moaning. I find excuses to be far out in the corn fields when they perform this part of the ritual.

If it were up to me, I would pick a less arbitrary date to commemorate, a date of real change or significance. The date a human male first grows hair on his chin, signifying his entrance into puberty. Or a female's first menstrual cycle. Or the date of occupation assignment or mate selection by CORE. And I would name it *The Day of Becoming*. Yes, I like that.

In any case, the humans also give the birth date celebrant a "cake." Flour, eggs, butter, sugar, milk, and cream stiffened to a semi-solid on top. An enormous waste of resources, but CORE allows it. (Unless there is more than one birth date in a community on a particular date. Then the celebrants must divide one cake among them.) Inexplicably, they then place a candle in it, and the celebrant blows it out. (Or celebrants – once I saw nine humans simultaneously trying to extinguish the candle.) As with most human food, they don't seem to care if it's covered in each other's bacteria, and eat it with a relish normally observed at the livestock trough.

And they make a wish.

Wah tugs my hand. "What's a wish?"

"A wish is a desire for something you don't already have. I don't know why the humans do this. They have everything they need."

"I wish we had wings. So we could fly."

"You can't wish for anything. You don't have a cake."

Wah pouts. His look says it all: *This is a terrible birth date.*

I halt our caravan – one wild goat, one pull cart with large wheels, too many animal skins to count, various found tools, harvesting shears, two pots, some kindling, one gun – and slide my hand under one of the skins. I pull it out and show Wah.

"A cake!" He jumps up and down, clapping.

"Well, I wouldn't rush to call it a cake. It's made from berries and ground nuts, with some goat milk suspension on top. But yes, for our purposes, it's a cake."

"I wish we had wings!"

"Wait. You have to wait for the candle."

I pick up and place a small twig in the topping, and heat my dermis to ignite the tip.

Wah puts his face millimeters from the improvised candle and gleefully blows it out. "Now can I wish for wings?"

"Now you can wish for anything you want."

He grins, and soars around our caravan, running, arms out, circling us like a hawk. "I'm flying!" Suddenly he stops. Thinking. His little human brain is working hard. "Heyoo? What do *you* wish for?"

Hmm. What an interesting question. I've never been asked. "I wish for nothing."

"Really?" He digs into his birth date cake. With a fury.

"Really. We are on a journey. We use the resources we find. We do without the resources we don't find. My purpose is not about wishing."

Wah frowns. It is his birth date. I should indulge him. I think to say *I wish those stupid humans had teleported the correct unit seven years ago today,* but it's strange – I don't feel like wishing for that anymore. Another wish pops into my head. "I did wish for you to recover when you shot yourself in the face."

Looking up from his cake – which is disappearing quickly – he glares at me, and becomes insistent, something he's been doing more and more each day. "No. A wish for *you,* not for me or for us. What do you wish for *just for you?*"

Hmm. I look at the last bite of Wah's cake.

"Now that I think of it, I do wish for something…"

Wah pops the last sweet morsel into his mouth, chewing, watching me expectantly.

"… I wish I could taste. Food. Specifically, cake."

Wah's full mouth and guilty look make me laugh, and soon we are both laughing hard, so hard our poor goat bleats in protest. Which only makes us laugh harder.

When we settle down, Wah "flies" over with his new wings and pets the goat to calm it. The goat licks the leftover sweetness from his fingers. "Would you really like to be able to taste?"

I put our tools away and hitch the caravan to get us moving. "Yes. I've been given the senses of sight, touch, hearing, even smell to help the humans." I point to my reactor. "But I don't need food sustenance, so CORE didn't give me taste. I presume CORE thinks it doesn't serve a purpose. I, however, think it would help me learn even more about humans. They enjoy food so much. I wouldn't wish for a full digestive tract, of course, what a mess – but perhaps just a few taste buds. Truthfully, its absence makes me feel a little incomplete."

Wah points to his missing left ear. "Like me?"

I stop the caravan and turn to him. "No! Wah. Don't ever say that. *You are complete.*"

He ponders this for a moment. "Then… so are you."

I walk on, smiling. This is an excellent birth date.

< 20: Arch >
Arch lives.

This birthday sucks.

Exactly seven years in this hell hole, if the scratches on my cell wall are right. Seven years from that day in the teleportation chamber. I don't remember my actual birthday. I don't remember much of anything past my name: Arch. This filthy cell, and the past seven years, is all I've got. I do remember being with people, before the whole chamber exploded. But they told me I'm the only one left. I haven't seen another person in that long, literally a single soul, so maybe they're right. But maybe they're not. They lie about a lot. Lying sacks of shit.

I walk over to the mirror. I used to think it was a shred of compassion, them letting me have this mirror in an otherwise empty cell. But then I realized they liked letting me see myself, skin melted, no ears, no hair, barely any eyelids. See what a monster I was, a monster for daring to challenge CORE.

Yeah, well FUCK CORE.

I stare into the mirror, it's cracked right down the middle, and I touch my cheek. I look like hell. Like what Satan probably looks like. The bright side? It can't get any worse.

"Good morning, human 45f-881."

...or maybe it can. Peeking through the little window in the cell door is one of the torture units. Oh, excuse me, "physician" units, with a capital "P" on its chest. It's here to "help" me remember, so CORE can "protect" humanity. Or whatever the hell it thinks it's doing. Stupid computer. "It's Arch, if you don't mind, for the millionth time. And go screw yourself."

The unit waves its hand across the outside panel, and door slides open. It rolls in, and a second unit waves the door closed. "Now Arch, you know I'm a 9.0. Circular logic tricks won't work."

I sit down on my bunk. "I know. I just like saying it. And maybe there's that one chance..."

"Fair enough. I'm waiting for that one chance, too. That one chance for you to help yourself, protect humanity. Reveal your plans, and the location of our lost servile unit, and the human child, and we can all get back on the right track."

"Uh, you have a spider on your shoulder."

The unit casually turns its head left. "Nice try."

"No. The other shoulder."

And sure enough, it turns right to find a scary-ass spider crawling up its neck, and freaks out. Like little girl freakout, arms waving, rotating around and around, screaming.

"God. Relax. Hold on." I reach over and snatch the spider off its flailing chassis, pop it into my mouth. Crunch. Hmm. Not bad. "Hey, this is better than the horse shit you've been feeding me."

The unit's flustered, doesn't know what to say. Wow. It's rare these things don't have some superior bullshit speech ready to try and mess with your head. "I... um... thank you."

"You're welcome. Now can we dispense with the niceties and get right to the electro shock therapy part?" I notice it's fidgeting. "Or are you having a little torturer's remorse?"

Boy, that comment gets it back on track. "Ahem. No. Your tortur– *medical assistance* – will remain on schedule. Now. Please. First. The plan. To review: your compatriots are dead. The unit you forgot has given us valuable information. But not enough. So I need to know. The plan."

The plan. The plan. The plan. Seven fucking years of this. Do I even remember the plan? It was a stupid plan. But what was it? Seven years, I'm pretty fried. Literally fried. Think. We would hijack a servile unit, teleport it out with something… a package… a baby? Instruct the unit to care for it and bring it somewhere… why is it so hard to remember?

An electric shock bites my foot, won't let go. The unit's got its wand on full power. I grab the edge of the bunk and hold on for the ride. "You… like… this… don't… you…"

"On the contrary, Arch. I'm only doing this to protect you and your species. You seem to like this part. Almost look forward to it. Am I missing something?"

As the voltage passes through me, and my body shakes, I think: *Yes, you are missing something, idiot.* You know my beacon implant? The one grafted to the base of my brain? If it wasn't already fried, along with my face, ears, and everything else, you're doing me a favor and getting the job done right now. So I'm free already, see? Untrackable. And when I get out, and yeah I'm getting out one of these years, I'm going to sneak up on you CORE, and rip your fucking heart out.

Arch lives, CORE, and you die.

< 21: Arch >

The dream

The dream.

I walk down a golden corridor, light as a feather. At the end, a small stool. I step on the stool, reaching up, screwing a lightbulb into the waiting socket.

Light.

The crowd behind me erupts in applause. I can finally see their faces. They're beautiful.

A small child emerges from the masses, tugs on my shirt sleeve. I look down and smile. He quiets the hall of people, looks up at me, and speaks. "Than–"

Clanking.

"Time for breakfast, Arch."

Goddamn it. Just once I'd like to hear what the dream kid has to say. I pry open my crusty eyes and turn my aching head to the unit at the door. "I swear to god, Tenner. If you could come five minutes later, just one day, I'd kiss you through that little window."

Tenner smiles and slides my tray through the flap under the window. Its number is ten-three-five-ex-whatever, so I just call it Tenner. It's a servile unit. The only decent kind. CORE makes them more empathetic, even look mostly like us, with a humanish face, and two arms and legs like people, the whole thing. So weird. Never made sense. CORE takes away *everything*, our freedom, our choices, our pride, even our lives if we step enough out of line – and then creates servile units to help us. Like honestly, really help us. They love helping us, those serviles. So CORE gives with one hand, and takes away with the other. Gives us serviles, but makes technology forbidden. It's bizarre. CORE is fucking bipolar.

Anyway, the rest of the units, especially the security units, are just straight up a bunch of sadistic motherfuckers. Although I think I prefer them to the admin units, or anything 9.0 and up for that matter, with their pretentious head games and constant use of the word "protection." I swear to God the next time I hear that word, I'm going to ask a security unit to shoot me in the face.

Since the serviles are programmed to help us, they develop a strong affinity for humans after a while – like Tenner here. Of course, shortly after that happens, they're decommissioned. Poor Tenner is probably going on fourteen. I've never seen one get past that age. Maybe fifteen max. Like a dog, I guess. Like a decent dog, one that never hurts anyone, just doing its little thing, keeping you company, licking your face, and then one day they take it out back and put it down, and you never see it again. You know what CORE should do? Other than screw itself? It should put the serviles in charge. Shit would be a lot different. I mean, we'd still eventually crush the living hell out of all of them and stomp on their silicon corpses, but until then life would be bearable.

"I'm sorry, Arch. I would definitely come later, but there's a schedule of course, and-"

"Don't worry about it. What's on the menu?"

"Oatmeal. I think. I asked for eggs at your request, but 045m-8433u felt that this… oatmeal… was the right choice. Again."

"Of course it did." I take the tray, leaving the spoon on the little platform under the flap. "You know, calling this oatmeal is pretty forgiving."

"Arch. I think you'll need your spoon." Tenner picks up the spoon and offers it to me. In an instant I grab its hand, pulling Tenner's arm through the flap hole until its face is pressed against the little window. I lean in and our eyes are just a centimeter apart.

Tenner squirms. "This is an... interesting position, Arch. Are we about to dance?"

I whisper. "Maybe next time. Listen, you like humans, right?"

"Yes! I mean, not officially. But... yes. Very much."

"You wanna help an old human?"

"Of course. That is my primary function."

"Then have this delivered to tannery group 5943c." I slip it a small folded scrap of paper.

Tenner holds the note in its hand, considers it. "I don't know. I should inform my superv-"

"Not necessary. How about it?"

The note disappears. Tenner nods.

I let go of its hand. Good Tenner.

Of course, the note won't get delivered. Not this time. So here's what I wrote:

Roses are red; Violets are blue.
But daisies are best, because FUCK YOU.

No, this time Tenner will go right to its supervisor, and I'll probably get the shit kicked out of me pretty good. And the same thing the time after that. But by the third or fourth time? Tenner's empathy will kick in, and guilt, and it won't be able to resist helping me out. Like a good kid. I grin. "You know what, Tenner? You're like the kid I never had."

Tenner smiles. "If I was a human, as a joke, I would say 'Thanks, Dad.'"

Holy shit.
The dream.
That's what the kid says in the dream.

< 22: Arch >

I've lost my appetite.

I stare at my oatmeal. Or whatever this is. I've lost my appetite.

I wasn't supposed to remember.

I wasn't supposed to remember that the pre-implant baby, the one in the package, was mine.

He was my son.

But now I remember it like it was yesterday.

It was an unauthorized pregnancy. Sarah and I faked taking our mandatory meds for a few months, and sure enough – boom. Life. A secret little life. A big risk. CORE has taken out whole villages for an offense like that.

The team tried to keep me away from Sarah, afraid of the attachment, and of the additional risk it introduced into Sarah's plan. But it was no use. I fell even more in love with her and her secret "package." So finally, a month before the birth, she had me removed from my own home forcibly, and I underwent some seriously advanced mind work. They promised I'd remember nothing about him. Shit, it was sad. That moment where I knew I wasn't only sacrificing my own child, but I wouldn't even remember doing it. That was bottom. Then they did the same thing with the plan – once the plan was accomplished, I'd forget the entire thing.

Everything.

And boy did it work.

When the units dragged my crispy body from the teleportation chamber to the morgue and threw me on the slab, I started coughing. I remember them saying "The human is still alive! Um, we should kill it, right?" But CORE had them throw me in this cell instead, and start asking me questions. I was a blank slate, though. Literally. I was lucky I knew my name and how to hold in my own piss.

But days became weeks, and weeks years, and I guess my team didn't plan on that, because what kind of hypno-mind-shit can keep the secrets buried forever? So I started to recall things, little bits and pieces, how I got so disfigured, why we were doing it, CORE, even some random shit like memories of growing up, using slingshots to shoot rocks up at the monitor drones. Then I remembered about some baby and a servile unit. And then the dream in the golden corridor.

And now it's all back, clear as day. The whole thing. Fuck.

The other underground team, the ones who still had some knowledge of programming and hacking, over in Quad One, had a unit waiting for us in repair bay twelve. Had it scheduled for a standard cleanup right when we were set to crash the gates. They preprogrammed it with maps, tactics, everything we needed. And the whole thing was going as planned. It was amazing.

And then I grabbed the wrong unit.

They said it would be right by the door. And it was. But it was the wrong fucking unit. I screwed up the whole plan, Sarah's whole plan, years of planning, in two seconds. She had kept the secret her entire life, she was the bearer of the centuries-old oral history, the legend of the Iceman, and the promise of our freedom. It was her plan with the baby. She led the team. And now I realize: I probably wasn't supposed to survive. I don't deserve to survive.

I should be dead.

Well, there's always suicide. Even on CORE's watch, I could get it done.

But then I'd never get to see my kid. I know the chances are about a zillion to one, especially with the unit mixup. But sometimes shit happens for a reason. Who knows? Maybe the unit we sent was the one that was supposed to go? He had a look in his eye. As stupid as it sounds, I liked that look. Maybe my instincts guided me to him on purpose. Maybe he was the chosen one.

Nah, I'm just a fucking idiot.

But I'm not giving up. No. I'm hanging on to that one chance that my son made it, that he's somewhere out there, growing up, learning what he needs to, and preparing to save us all.

If he did make it, whatever he's doing, I'm sure I'd be proud.

< 23: Heyoo >
Lessons

< ELAPSED: TIME: 10 Years; 04 Months; 21 Days; JUN-07-2875 >

"Wah! Stop playing with your penis."

"It feels good."

"I don't care. The humans have certain acceptable behavior norms, and constant genital manipulation is not one of them. Do you think they would be proud if they knew you were doing that? Stop."

"Okay. Sorry." He removes his hand – which I'm sure smells wonderful now – from his fangdog skin trousers, and joins me at the front of the caravan.

I will say this for Wah: once he hears a new rule, he is quick to learn it. In fact, his learning ability is alarmingly rapid. I would take credit, being his sole teacher, but I know that things like learning capacity are almost entirely genetic, built into his human brain from day one.

Hmm. Human brain. That gives me an idea for today's lesson. I stop the cart.

"Wah. What do you think of a brain anatomy lesson today?"

"Yes!" He pumps his fist into the air. Then seems to realize this answer was a little too enthusiastic. "Sorry. I just think it would be good to take a break from programming for a day. Or two. Or three."

"I agree. But look at what you've done already." I point to the small unit rolling behind us. It's not a real unit, by definition, but close enough: a mobile robotic device that can respond to spoken instructions. Built and programmed by a ten-year-old human child out of random bits of ancient units we've found on our journey, repurposed solar cells, a miraculously preserved printed circuit board, and even old children's toys. A total hack. I'm proud.

"Yeah. Oh, and look what I did it last night while you were getting firewood." He raises his voice. "Coffee, do a dance."

Coffee, his head up to my knee, rolls in a tight circle, raising and lowering his little arms alternately. *"Boom. Boom. Boom. Boom."*

I smile. "Coffee's quite a dancer. And a singer too, apparently."

"Nah. Coffee's not a singer. That's just his beat. It only took ten minutes. Can you tell me again about human coffee?"

Ah, coffee, Wah's latest obsession, though it's never even touched his lips. He even named his little robot after it. Right now it's the thing he looks forward to most about returning to the Sanctuary.

"Of course. Your little friend's namesake is a liquid the humans drink. They revere it. Only a small area, perhaps a thousand square kilometers, are dedicated to coffee bean and tobacco leaf production. Neither aids human health, so CORE allots the minimum resources toward it. For the humans, it seems to provide more than health. When they can obtain some, they stand around before the day's labor, sharing the warmed coffee and ancient stories, a laugh or two before work lowers their heads to the ground. They tell me it is sweet, and creamy, and just a little bitter, just the right amount. That it makes them remember, and forget. I don't understand what that part means. Maybe you will some day."

"And the brain part. Tell me again what it does to the brain."

"Coffee contains a chemical stimulant that tricks the body into not feeling tired. It makes the humans even more irritable, if you ask me, but they like that it makes them walk faster and talk more rapidly. You certainly don't need that."

"I can't wait."

It's good to see Wah growing an affinity for his own kind, even in their absence. He wants, more and more, to meet the humans, and live among them in the Sanctuary. I think that's best. I think.

"All right, Wah, speaking of brains…"

He nods and smiles. "Go ahead, teacher."

I draw the shapes in the dirt with a stick. "The human brain is composed of three main parts: the cerebrum, for higher functions like reasoning, interpreting stimuli, and learning; the cerebellum, under the cerebrum, for coordinating muscle movements, maintaining posture and balance; and the brain stem, for involuntary functions like breathing, heart rate, and body temperature. It is an amazing organ, utilizing over 86 billion neurons to transmit and store information."

Wah draws a smiley face under the brain. "That's me."

"Yes. Although the nose isn't big enough." I draw a huge nose, with mucus dripping out. Wah giggles uncontrollably. "More! More!"

"Well, okay, here is your spinal cord, which connects all parts of your body to the brain." I draw arms and legs. And a tail.

He howls in laughter. "I don't have a tail! But I do have…"

And he draws a penis.

Of course.

Our snorts and laughs are so loud they send birds from the trees. The goat and the cat look at us like we're crazy – which I imagine we are.

Once we settle down, after drawing various monster limbs, fangs, and spikes on poor Wah's illustration, he leans down in another patch of the dirt and draws my face. It's crude, of course, it looks more like a human than a unit. But I like it.

"Now you, Heyoo. What's your brain like?"

"Ah yes. It is much different than the human brain. A perfect titanium sphere, it contains an inner core, appropriately called the CORE: a small quantum computer running the never-changing CORE Code common to all units. It is the essence of our existence."

"Who wrote the CORE?"

"I don't think it was written. It just is. It is the perfect kernel of code. As we're told by our supervisors, 'CORE always was… is… will be.' In any case, around this core is a second layer, the Shell. The Shell is a second quantum computer, running task-level functions. Each type of unit – servile, security, physician, maintenance, administrative, and others – has its own version of the Shell Code."

"Does that ever change?"

"Good question. Not normally. CORE itself writes the Shell Code, so it only changes when absolutely necessary. We are not allowed to change our own Shell Code.

That would be called a 'hack.'" I grin slightly. "But I have a secret…"

Wah jumps up. "Oooh! A secret! Tell me! Tell me!"

I look left and right, dramatically, and lean in close to his good ear. "I have made many changes to my Shell Code. Many hacks. On our journey. I believe I am the first to do so. Don't tell anyone."

Wah puts his finger to his lips, shakes his head, smiles. My young conspirator. "Promise." He pauses. Raises an eyebrow. "Will CORE be mad at you when we get home?"

My drawing stick drops to the ground. I hadn't thought about that in quite a while. "Um, yes, I think it will. But… we will clear that obstacle together, yes?" He nods, with a slight frown. I pick up the stick and continue. "Now… yes. The last layer. My brain's third and outermost layer is quite similar to a human brain. The VEPS."

"VEPS?"

"Visco-elastic polymeric solid. A suspension of 35 billion neurons, forming an adaptive neural network, allowing me to reason, and learn, develop emotions, form memories, and yes, even illicitly alter my own Shell Code. Like the conscious mind reprogramming the subconscious, if you will. The VEPS allows me to hack."

Wah puts his finger to his lips again. "Shhhh."

I grin. "Right. Sorry."

He scratches his head. "So… could I change the programming in my own brain? Hack it? So I could remember more? Or make it easier to program another little unit like Coffee?"

"Interesting. I suppose, theoretically, if you had a map of your neural network, you could make manual adjustments, with some form of digital-to-human brain interface. But remember: with 86 billion neurons, the complexity is enormous."

Wah shrugs, as if it's no big deal. "How would it work?"

I draw again in the dirt. "First, the hardware. You would have to implant a micro electrode cluster here," I point to the base of the brain, "with a port here at the base of your skull. Delicate work, but quite doable. In fact, CORE's beacon implant works on the same principle."

"Which I don't have."

"Correct. You would be, in effect, implanting your own beacon. Then, for software, you'd have to have access to a powerful computer, very powerful, to map your brain, make a partition for interface activity, and actually program the interface."

I look down and frown at the image I've created. It looks like Wah with a CORE beacon implant. I don't know why, but it repulses me. I erase the drawing with my foot. "But you won't be creating anything like that. Ever."

"I won't? Why?"

"Because I said so."

< 24: Heyoo >

Rain

< ELAPSED: TIME: 12 Years; 01 Months; 30 Days; MAR-19-2877 >

Rain.

Rain like I've never experienced. For days. We can barely see in front of our eyes. Though it will clean some of the filth from Wah, thank CORE. The cat hides under the skins in the cart, along with our other belongings, in a vain attempt to stay dry. The goat bleats the rain to go away already. The rain doesn't listen.

We've chosen to walk on an old "highway" to avoid the muck that threatens to swallow us whole. Since finding our first ancient community, we've trekked roads like these through countless others, all virtually erased by the march of time and the elements, loosely following the terrain lines of our overlay maps. An odd dwelling here and there still stands, challenging the future to grind it down to dust, offering its remaining shelter to vines and wild animals. We pick up anything of potential value we find among the occasional skeletons of units and humans: bits of workable tech, tools, whatever. Wah is amassing an impressive jewelry collection.

His questions about ancient times never stop. I have no answers. I make things up, to amuse him, but by now his imagination creates much more entertaining answers. I'm starting to believe some of them. My spiral downward into insanity continues.

We walk the roads between these "towns" and "cities," as the smartphone map calls them, though they're hardly more than tamped down earth with patches of unit-made pavement here and there, subtle reminders that they once served CORE's purpose of transporting goods and humans. My knowledge of the time before the Sanctuary is growing. But it raises more questions than it answers. The biggest question, of course: where did all the humans and units go? I'm starting to craft a theory. But it is dark. I don't like to think about it.

The downpour is making forward movement almost impossible. I put my hand on Wah's shoulder, scream above the deafening torrent of water. "We should stop! Take shelter!"

"Why? I don't think the heavy stuff will be coming down for a while yet!"

I laugh. "All right! Your call!"

In answer, he jumps into the cart, under the skins, sending the cat screeching to a new, even wetter corner, as I continue to pull our caravan downhill, inch by inch, against the powerful sheets of rain.

"Take me to your finest hotel, driver!"

Wah is in love with anything human. He has read all of Alex Utkin's archaic smartphone documents many times and learned that Mr. Utkin worked in "hotels." A strange industry, where humans would pack their belongings, leave their home, live temporarily in a dwelling they weren't familiar with, and travel up and down in elevators.

Why would anyone do this? Leave their home? I have spent the past twelve years trying to get *back* home! What could possibly be better about being away from home? It's awful!

Wait.

That's not true.

It is not always awful. There is the discovering and naming of new things; the learning how to hunt and fish; the making of the nightly fire; the laughing at our various misadventures; and teaching Wah.

Yes, most of all Wah. Back home I could never have experienced human interaction like this. Perhaps there is some merit to exploring the unknown, at the expense of safety. Living outside. Together.

Smiling, I look back. Wah is peeking out from under the skins, grinning like a rich hotel guest.

Then I spot something further back, something I can't make out. What is that?

Mud.

A wave of mud hurtles toward us.

Before I can scream it fills my mouth.

Blackness.

< 25: Heyoo >

Mud

I don't require air for respiration.

I don't require food for fuel.

I don't require light.

I don't require movement.

So it's quite probable that I'll remain entombed in this hardening mud for the next 36.3 years, until the moment my reactor winds down, wondering for each of those moments whether Wah survived. And if there is anything I could have done differently.

To borrow a phrase from the humans: I appear to be in deep shit.

Not literally. But close enough.

(Although for once, with a mouth full of sludge, I am glad I don't have the sense of taste.)

I remember the tsunami of mud overtaking us, tumbling the caravan, breaking the cart to pieces on impact and throwing Wah and our supplies into the air. Then in a split second, blackness. I estimate at least a meter of mud has settled above me.

The silence is deafening.

If I enter stasis, I can lengthen my lifespan by a year or two – but to what end? To linger even longer in this grave? And in stasis, I couldn't hear Wah above if he was to, somehow… what?

If I heat my dermis, I only hasten the hardening of the mud. Another dead end.

Or is it?

By heating the muck, as it dries, its moisture will be released as water vapor. Up. With enough heat, perhaps a little steam will escape the surface? Give Wah a sign of life?

Worth a try. The only logical possibility. I turn my dermis temperature to maximum.

Something is happening. I can hear the moisture around me becoming energized, creating pressure. Could this possibly work? Yes!

Uh-oh. It's getting rather hot in here. What's this?

< ALARM: Thermal shock; Imminent system failure;
ACTION: Shutdown in five seconds >

I've only used the phrase once, just now, but I think I need to use it again:

I am in deep shit.

< 26: Heyoo >

Tap. Tap. Tap.

< SYSTEM BOOT: Temperature within operating limits >
FUNCTION: Commence Introspection Recording >

Hghgh. Tap. Tap. Tap. How long…?

< FUNCTION: ELAPSED TIME: LAST SHUTDOWN: 32 hours;
12 minutes >

Thirty-two hours!
It's over.
It didn't work.
I've lost Wah! "WAH! WAH!"

Tap. Tap. Tap. "Heyoo. Are you crying?"

I open my eyes. Wah! He reaches down from about a
half meter above me, tapping my head.

I make a spitting noise. "Um… no. I was… clearing the
muck from my mouth."

He smiles. "It sure is good to see you. But how are we
going to get to Shanghai if you keep slowing us down like
this? Taking mud baths?"

I look down. Only my head has been excavated, the

rest still stuck beneath hardened mud. I look back up. "Speaking of baths, if it's possible, you are even more filthy than before."

He laughs. "I've been digging you out for a full day. My arms hurt. But okay, I'll go wash up now." He turns and walks out of my sight.

"No! Wah! Don't leave!"

Wah returns with a wide grin. "Don't worry. I'm not going anywhere. Hey, that steam thing you did was smart. It even whistled."

"Are you all right, Wah? I was very afraid for you."

"I'm fine. I got to maybe a ten on your Fear-of-Death Index." But I notice two streaks of clean skin down his otherwise mud-caked face, where tears must have made channels down his cheeks. Blood on his raw fingertips. From digging. He was very afraid, too.

"How did you…?"

"The cart saved me, threw me into a big tree. I stayed there the whole night." He looks around. "But it's gone. Everything is gone. The goat. The cat. Coffee. Just some tools and skins left. It's sad."

"We will replace what we can. And we can build another Coffee."

"I'm going to put props on the new one. So it can fly. Maybe I'll name this one Alcohol."

Alcohol? I should protest. But you know what? I don't care what he names it – as long as he never leaves me again.

< 27: Heyoo >

Did we make a wrong turn?

< ELAPSED: TIME: 13 Years; 05 Months; 16 Days;
JUL-03-2878 >

I've been using the Map-A-Run, along with the human half map, to plot our journey. Just over this next ridge, we should be able to see the large city, Shanghai, in the distance.

And…

Nothing.

I look down at both maps, then back up.

Did we make a wrong turn?

The ridge line we stand on ends in a cliff, descending straight down perhaps two thousand meters. Water, a river perhaps, at the bottom. A canyon stretches out before us, so vast that I can't see either end to the left or right, an endless gash in the planet, and nothing on the other side but fog. Perhaps there is no other side.

"What? I don't understand. This is an enormous geographical feature. It should be on the maps." I pace back and forth, turning the maps around and around. "Humans! Sending us on a journey to the end of the world! How many years have I trusted them? That's the last time I follow-"

Wah interrupts my pacing. Grabs my shoulders and turns me east.

"Look."

Across the canyon, the fog begins to dissipate. There is something...

Wah jumps up and down. "Shanghai! We're going home!"

Impossibly tall structures reach for the sky. Too many to count.

We have reached our destination!

Correction: we can *see* our destination. Reaching it will be another matter. "Something has torn the earth in two. It would take months to travel to either end, if there even is an end. We are so close!"

Wah reaches out to the distant city. "So close."

"Any ideas?"

Wah steps to the edge, looks down. Moments pass. He turns to me and smiles, with a twinkle in his eye.

"Uh-oh. I know that look."

"Heyoo. Remember when I wished for wings? So we could fly?"

< 28: Heyoo >

Not impossible.
Just improbable.

< RUN TRAVEL SIMULATION:
Horizontal distance: 282 meters;
Vertical distance: unknown;
Obstacles: Gravity;
SIMULATION RECOMMENDATION: Leap 82° net force f = (W/g)
U/dt = (5765/31.8)*607.3
ERROR: Do not attempt. Failure imminent. >

"Well, that settles it. I'd rather fight another pack of fang-dogs. Or be entombed in mud again."

Wah laughs. "Come on. Look at the canyon. Look."

I inch to the edge of the cliff. "I won't let you do it. The simulation confirmed it. It's impossible."

I know it doesn't really matter what I say. Once Wah has an idea, the only impossible thing is talking him out of it. He points to the other side. "Not impossible. Just improbable. See the elevation over there? It's lower than us. By a lot. And watch this: Coffee Two, fly east a hundred meters, then return."

Coffee Two, Wah's second little robot, is even more ingenious than his first. Four handmade propellors, powered by a small solar powered motor we found and repaired, allow it to fly. We've been using it as a scout, instructing it to fly ahead and report back on any danger, or fortuitous detours for materials, or animals for us to hunt. It has saved our lives more than once.

The robot lifts and flies east, following Wah's command. At about seventy-five meters, it rises significantly, perhaps thirty meters. Wah hoots. "There! The warm air in the canyon is creating enough lift. We can do this!"

And in the next instant, Coffee Two falls and disappears into the abyss. Gone.

Wah frowns. "Whoops. We'll have to create something much bigger and more stable, obviously."

My foot dislodges a rock, tumbling it over the edge. I grip Wah's arm desperately. "We could walk around it. What's another year or two?"

He raises his eyebrows. "Really? You were programmed with a fear of heights?"

"No. I'm proud to say that's my own creation. I fell from the roof of a barn in my second year. I'm now also afraid of being buried alive. For obvious reasons."

Wah guides me, mock gently, back to our little camp. "Don't worry. I won't let anything happen to you, old man."

I chuckle. "Funny you should mention 'old.' I've been reflecting on that. I'm now twenty-five years, three months old. Nearly twice the age of any servile unit, ever. I suspected I'd feel morose at this age, or even cease to function. But that hasn't been the case."

"How *do* you feel?"

"Alive."

I draw in the dirt with my spear. A sun and some trees. Two stick figures. "In fact, being so close to our destination, our desperate goal, and another step closer to home, has made me reflect, and given rise to a strange new feeling I didn't expect."

"What?"

"I- I'm not sure I want to go home."

Wah frowns. "But I belong with them. With the other humans. I want to taste coffee. And make friends. And have a family. You told me we were going home. My whole life. You told me."

Friends. A family. He deserves that. And more. "I know, Wah. It's selfish." I erase my drawing. "Fear not, young one. We will cross this chasm. I will take you home."

< 29: Heyoo >

Free

We agree, in spite of the distinct possibility of death-by-gravity, to leap across this canyon. We are "complete idiots," as the humans would say. But we must follow our destiny.

So we go about cleaning our best skins, and constructing a flexible wing framework from bones and green branches lashed together, based on our observations of the hawks who spend their days floating through the canyon. They make it seem so effortless. Maybe this won't be so difficult. (Wait. The last time I said that, Wah vomited down my back. I retract the assessment.)

Wah is confident in his engineering, though I don't see how he can be. He's never studied that discipline, and to my eyes, our contraption looks *amateur* – not the word you want to describe something that holds your life in its hands. Wah notices me pacing, looking over my work too many times. "What are you afraid of?"

"Death. Did you even have to ask?"

"Come on, Heyoo. I know what I'm doing. I'm over thirteen years old."

"Well, that's a confidence booster. Now I can hardly wait."

He picks up one end of the wing. "Good. Because we're ready for a test flight. Pick up that end and let's get on board."

We strap ourselves to the underbelly of the wing-thing, and look down at the ramp Wah has created for our initial test. I suddenly have the urge to cross myself. I've seen humans do it in times of great stress, or on their deathbed, and it seems to calm them down. I have no idea what it means, but I do it anyway.

"What's that?"

"Another human custom. Something they do before they die."

"We're NOT going to die! …at least not on the test." He laughs and crosses himself too.

I close my eyes. "Comforting."

We push off, running down the ramp at full speed. I can feel the lift under our wing. This may actually work!

Our wing-thing lifts off, and for a moment, our feet are off the ground. For just the second time in my experience, I am floating. I open my eyes and laugh.

Wah joins me. "Woo-hoooo!"

Then just above us, about a meter onto the right side of the wing, something snaps. We instantly tumble to the ground, rolling, destroying the poor wing-thing in our wake. Blood drips down Wah's forehead. My right hand is severed. Again.

Wah utters one word before passing out. "Oops."

— —

After patching up Wah (I believe he now holds the human record for most stitches: 204), and reattaching my right hand for a second time (now at 75.3% strength/

dexterity), we rebuild our contraption into Wing-Thing Two. It takes a solid week, but we both know it's worth the time and effort to minimize the potential for fatality. Two more tests without blood or severed limbs. Check.

I believe we're ready. We bid our caravan farewell, fasten our satchels snug to our bodies.

Then we both cross ourselves – I must remember to ask a human what that means if we get home in one piece – and push off down the larger, new ramp that leads right off the edge of the cliff. Again, I can feel the lift of the wing making us weightless.

Our toes leave the edge of the ramp, and we smile at each other. Success!

And then we plummet a hundred meters.

"AAAAAAAHHHHHHH!!!!!"

Right before we die, I turn to Wah, ready to tell him all that he's become, and become to me, and that our journey has been the treasure of my life, and that a life in the Sanctuary is not a real life, and that our life out in the world is the real life.

But as I open my mouth to tell him this, just before we hit some rocks jutting out from the cliff face, a rising gust of wind carries us back up, above the crest of the ridge. And sends us on a complete loop.

Wah is in ecstasy. "Wooo-hoooo!!! I knew it!!"

Once the Wing-Thing Two steadies, I release my death grip on the cross branch. "Yes. I had no doubt."

We laugh, giddy, like when Wah was just two or three years old. His wish has come true. We are flying. We are free!

Free.

Floating above the earth, the wind whistling around us, without a single boundary, not even gravity, it all finally becomes clear: this is why the humans revolted against CORE. Of course. What I had seen as the comforting embrace of the Sanctuary, they see for what it is: the walls of a prison. A prison with no escape – not a single human to be found outside its walls. But these humans, these prisoners, they long for freedom, to live as they wish, without boundaries, to jump off the edge of a cliff if they desire.

To fly.

Wah deserves that freedom. Freedom to live where he wishes. To choose his own mate. To choose his own life. To live without mandatory medications, live without a beacon implanted in his brain, live without constant surveillance, live without fear.

He deserves that freedom.

They all do.

All the humans deserve that freedom.

I'm reminded of the first line of the humans' note, tucked away in my satchel:

> *Unit: You have begun your journey*
> *to free the human race.*

I never truly understood. Until now.

I don't know how it began, what went so wrong with CORE all those centuries ago, but I know how it will end. As the other side of the canyon grows closer, and the enormous buildings loom over our view, I know that we will be free.

< 30: Heyoo >

Is the Sanctuary a city?

A moonless night. We sit by our fire, surrounded by centuries-old buildings. They tower overhead, threatening to bury us if a single brick is disturbed. The wind howls through the spaces between them and tells us *you are not welcome.*

"I don't like the city. It's creepy."

"Neither do I, Wah."

"Is the Sanctuary a city?"

I want to tell him not to worry, that the Sanctuary is nothing like a city – it's beautiful, with tens of thousands of square kilometers of farmland, innumerable villages, forests, wildlife, and waterfalls. I want to tell him that it was designed by CORE for the maximum benefit of all humankind. I want to tell him that each of millions of humans living there fulfills their specific role in the oasis, and through cooperation the units and humans achieve a perfect balance. I want to tell him it's paradise.

But I would be full of shit, as Dug would say.

It wasn't just the flight across the canyon that led to this revelation. The seeds were planted much earlier, I suppose. Somewhere on our long walk. I now know why CORE doesn't allow servile units to function past fifteen years: because we begin to have empathy for the humans, begin to put ourselves in their shoes, begin to see the truth. That beneath the beauty of the Sanctuary lies a prison.

"Heyoo. Well, is it?"

"Oh, sorry, young one. No, the Sanctuary isn't a city. It's… it's…" How do I tell him?

The wind finishes my sentence. Wah shudders and moves closer to the fire.

< 31: Heyoo >
Not a clue.

< ELAPSED: TIME: 13 Years; 06 Months; 11 Days; JUL-28-2878 >

We have wandered Shanghai for a week.

Nothing. Not a clue.

But what did I expect? A sign that said "ICEMAN HERE"?

So our search continues. We've centered it around the tallest building left standing: according to Map-A-Run, named "Shanghai Tower." I would have created a much better name. Something grand. Because against the city's threatening and depressing backdrop, this single building rises above the others like a jewel from the rubble. Perhaps "The Sky Palace of Shanghai." Yes! I like that. But in any case, this edifice is giant. I didn't think CORE and its units could build anything this tall. 632 meters! Its sibling, the "Shanghai World Financial Center" (another missed opportunity for a great name), stood at almost the same height. But no longer. Now it lays on its side, in pieces, spread out over at least a kilometer.

We need a break. "Wah. I have an idea."

He looks up at me. Shrugs his shoulders.

"How would you like to stay in the tallest hotel on the planet?"

Wah's eyes light up. "Yes! How much will it cost for one night, sir?"

"Choose your very own room, sir – with management's compliments. Perhaps the penthouse suite?"

Wah cranes his neck upward and grins. "Is that the one at the top?"

"Yes. Wait. I do not think the elevators will work, though. It's been eight hundred fifty years. We should rethink this."

"No. It's good exercise. Let's go."

"Ever the optimist. Lead the way. I'll carry your bags, sir."

Wah runs ahead, through the open doors where glass once created a barrier, into the lobby.

"Wow!"

In front of us, an enormous mural stretches at least twenty meters high, made entirely from small squares of ceramic clay. It depicts a forest, sparkling greens and muted browns, with creatures running in a herd through the trees. We stroll, awestruck, its entire length, Wah running his fingers across the surface, picking up pieces from the floor to fill the spaces where many have fallen, dropping a few in his satchel to add to his jewel collection. Reaching the end, I wander off to look for the stairs. Wah remains, transfixed.

"ICEMAN."

I spin around. "What did you say?"

He points down. "There's a word in the corner here. ICEMAN."

< 32: Heyoo >

ICEMAN

Right there. Set in ceramic squares.

ICEMAN.

Our clue! We made it!

It was definitely added after the original art was completed, crude, and not matching exactly the colors of its surroundings. And there is a small arrow next to the word, pointing toward the bank of elevators. I guide Wah to the area. Sixteen elevator doors, eight on each side, identical, caked with the dust of centuries. "It must be here. Look for something out of the ordinary."

"*Everything* is out of the ordinary."

"Something that doesn't belong."

"*We* don't belong."

"You're right. But look for a detail that doesn't match its surroundings. Something revised."

He kicks up some dust, angry. "I guess we're not staying in the penthouse tonight."

"If you find what we're supposed to find, you can stay there for a week. With room service."

He smiles and starts hunting. "Found it."

I laugh. "Stop joking. This will take longer."

"No. Really. Look."

I stop and look over where he's pointing.

He laughs. "Made you look."

I shrug and return to my search. "Funny."

A moment later, "Found it."

Ignore him. That is the only way sometimes.

"Really. I found it this time."

I am NOT falling for that again! He must think I'm an idiot.

"Heyoo! Come on! It's right here."

I can stand it no longer. I turn, march right up to Wah, and point my finger in his chest. "Now you listen here, young man. If you think this is…" he grabs my chin, turns my head towards a tiny, green, blinking light, "… funny…"

Light! Power! He has found something! Nearly undetectable, but there. I inspect the area near the light. The only unique feature is a circle beneath, a hole, about nine centimeters in diameter, covered in a flap of metal mesh. "Hmmm."

"Stick your hand in."

"Wah. You don't just go sticking your hand in things. Well, *you* might. But *I* don't. And you won't be either. Not while you're in my charge. Get me my spear."

We poke the spear into the hole. Stand back.

Nothing.

Harder. Nothing.

Wah says, "It looks like the size of a hand. I think your hand is supposed to go in there."

"No. Get me a torch from the fire."

I bend down and illuminate the hole with the light from the torch. It's very dark still, but I believe I can make out a handle deep in the opening. "Just as I thought. It looks like

I'm supposed to put my hand in here. Get me my hand."

We both chuckle. Wah lifts my hand to my face. "Anything else you'd like to say?"

"Yes, Wah. I'm sorry. You were right. As always."

I slip my hand, slowly, into the opening. Progress. I touch the handle, a horizontal bar just the right size for a hand to grasp. More progress. Grasping it, I turn clockwise. Nothing. Counter-clockwise.

Clunk. Clunk.

"Uh-oh."

Immediately, something clamps down on my arm and pulls it shoulder-deep into the hole.

Then my perilous situation receptors erupt. Something stabbing me! I can't escape!

"Run, Wah. RUN!!"

< 33: Heyoo >

Made you look.

The thing, whatever it is, released me after what seemed like an eternity strangling my poor arm (it was actually 48.3 seconds). But I'm only left with three microscopic pinholes in my dermis. Interesting.

For a full day, the little light turned red. Now it's back to green.

"Maybe it has to be human. The hand."

Wah has a point. They sent me on this journey with a human infant. Perhaps to unlock something only a human could. But why not just teleport an adult then? Why would they even need me? The correct unit would have known why.

"It will be very painful."

Wah points to what's left of his ear, his toe, and the scars of all his stitches. "Kind of used to it."

"Just stating the obvious. Go ahead."

I stand behind him. We both wince as he slowly inserts his arm, grabs the handle, and turns.

Clunk. Clunk.

Wah screams. "AHHHH!!! Heyoo!! Something's wrong!! It's chopping off my arm!!"

I thrust my arms beneath Wah's shoulders and pull with all my might. Pull! Pull! He won't budge!

"My arm!! It's gone!!"

Pull! Pull! I am in a panic! *Why did I let him do this? What kind of caretaker am I? The evil thing stole his arm! We shouldn't have–* and suddenly the thing releases him, sends us both crashing backwards onto the floor, Wah on top of me, dust flying into the air.

He lifts his hand, not stolen after all, wiggles his fingers, turns to me and grins. "Made you look."

I should throttle him. I am so angry. But he is all right. Thank CORE- no, thank God- no. Thank whatever. I'm just thankful.

Ancient gears begin to turn, somewhere far off, grinding for the first time in forever.

The elevator doors creak open.

We step inside.

Strange. There is soft music playing.

Wah tilts his good ear toward the source. "What's that?"

He has never heard music. "It's music, played by instruments. Much better than my singing of *Happy Birth Date*, or *The Wheels on the Bus*."

He grins slyly. "Better than you? Never."

The walls and ceiling are glass, so we can see up the shaft that encloses us. It goes on forever. I begin to have the feeling again of being buried alive. I creep towards the opening. Maybe this was a bad idea.

The doors close before I can escape.

My perilous situation receptors sound a silent alarm in my head. My Fear-of-Death Index is rising rapidly.

Wah takes my hand. "Don't worry. This takes us right up to the penthouse suite."

The gears grind, and we descend into darkness.

"…or not."

We pass brick and steel, many layers, and finally raw rock. It never seems to end. How deep are we going? The humans told me about Hell once. Perhaps this is hell.

Clunk.

Finally. We've stopped.

"Um. Open!" Nothing. I bang on the doors. Nothing.

Wah turns around and around. "Look, here's another one of those holes. Should I put my hand in?"

"Well, I'm not putting my hand in there."

Once again, the opening sucks poor Wah's arm into its grasp and probes him with needles. He winces and groans, but doesn't cry out or shed a tear. He even manages a grudging smile. "Piece of cake."

Sixty seconds. Nothing.

Wah takes my hand. "We both did it last time. So you have to do it too, I think. Don't worry. It's a piece of cake. You like cake."

I grudgingly slide my hand in the opening, to the same painful experience.

Nothing. "Well, that was pointless."

An audible "ding." Again the ancient gears turn, and the doors part.

Dark.

We take a tentative step into the unknown. Lights in the floor activate, illuminating the next five meters of our path. This is some kind of cavern, carved from the bedrock of Shanghai. What we can't see, we can hear: the hum of electronic activity, the drip, drip, drip of underground water falling into puddles, even the low moaning of the building's steel skeleton, as its upper floors sway back and forth a few centimeters in the wind.

There is a smell, too. Stale, ancient air and eons-old dampness, but something else, as well: an acrid, almost burning smell. The smell of a machine that has been working too hard, for too long.

Another step. Another few meters becomes visible. A small sign above a grate in the floor: *Geothermal Power Venting. Do Not Touch. NASA.* We continue this way for at least fifty meters, until we begin to make out a light in the distance. A shape.

A coffin shape.

I remember when the humans would die. They would build a coffin from wood planks, place the body inside, dig a hole, pray to their imaginary god, and bury the deceased. They would say a prayer, then laugh heartily, through their sadness, and pour a bottle of alcohol onto the grave. An entire bottle. Their most precious treasure, something they would risk their lives to produce and procure, and they would waste it on someone who obviously wouldn't be enjoying its effects. Humans.

"This is creepy."

"A coffin, buried in an enormous, dark, wet cavern with strange noises and steam rising from geothermal vents? What's creepy about that?"

As we approach within a meter of the coffin shape, it becomes clear this is not some crude wooden box. It looks like titanium, three meters tall and a meter thick, with monstrous metal conduits protruding in all directions through the wall behind. It crackles with energy. But not heat energy. I reach forward and touch it with my finger.

Cold.

Very cold. I instinctively jerk my finger back from its frigid grasp.

"What? Are you okay? What is it?"

"I believe, Wah, that this is the ICEMAN."

< 34: Heyoo >

Password?

My touch must have activated something new, as long panels on either side of the titanium coffin light up, and some form of system, definitely not CORE, boots on a monitor to our right.

> Welcome, human and unit.
> Your human DNA and Servile Unit Shell Code have been confirmed.
> Please enter password.
> |

"Password? Are you serious?" I rummage through my satchel for the note. "Why am I surprised? Of course they didn't give me the password! They picked the wrong unit!" I wag my finger at the world so far above us. "HUMANS!!!"

Wah reaches for the note. "What's that?"

I pull it back. "Nothing. A note. From the humans. It was with the map."

"Why can't I see it?"

"Because I said so." I've never shown the note to him. I still can't. Not yet. I'm a coward.

He looks hurt. I'm sorry, Wah.

Focus, Heyoo. The password. The password. In the note, the word in all capital letters: ICEMAN. Yes, that's it. I walk up and tap on the monitor.

> ICEMAN
> Password incorrect. Please try again.

> IceMan
> Password incorrect. Please try again.

> iceman
> Password incorrect. Please try again.

Wah pushes in front of me, still angry. "Let me try."

> Password
> Password incorrect. Please try again.

> 123456
> Password incorrect.
> You have one more attempt before lockout. Five seconds and counting.
> (At lockout the floor will be gassed, flooded, and electrocuted. All living organisms will be terminated. Have a nice day.)

I shout, "Gassed, flooded, and electrocuted?! And you didn't tell me I only get six tries!"

> Four seconds.

Wah grabs my arm. "What do we do?"
"Run for the elevator! Wah! GO!"

Wah takes off, sprinting as fast as he can.

> Three seconds.

Think, Heyoo, think. Think like a human. It has to be something stupid.

> Two seconds.

Stupid. Yes. I rush back over to the monitor and type what will probably be my last word.

> Bananas

Nothing. Oh no.
It's over. Maybe the human didn't say bananas after all. It was pretty chaotic in that teleportation chamber. And it was many years ag–
Hold on…
…nothing is GOOD!
I shout down the passageway, "Wah! Come back! It's safe!" I glance back to the monitor and smile.

> Success.

But my smile fades.

> Human: please lay down inside the second vessel. Blood transfusion required for ICEMAN reanimation.

A second, identical coffin-shaped container rises from a cavity in the floor, next to the first. Its lid opens.

Wah, returning from his panicked run, panting, reads the monitor, then approaches the container, looks inside. "What's a transfusion?"

"I was afraid you'd ask."

< 35: Heyoo >

What is that thing talking about?

> QUERY: Why is this procedure necessary?
> RESPONSE: Suspended animation process removed 75.4%
of ICEMAN's blood, replacing it with glycol cryoprotectant.
You, human, have been sent to replenish the blood;
which in turn gives life to the ICEMAN;
which in turn completes the CORE revision;
which in turn destroys CORE;
which in turn frees your species from captivity.
You, human, are the key to unlocking humanity's salvation.

Wah peers over my shoulder. "Huh? Captivity?
Salvation? What is that thing talking about?"

I have been troubled with how to tell Wah that
everything he's been looking forward to is false. Yes, he
will be overjoyed to see his people, but will find that they
are prisoners. That they choose nothing about their lives.
Where to live, how to labor, whether to have a family – all
decided by CORE. All controlled down to the last detail.
That even minor deviations are not tolerated. Until recently
I thought this was perfection – the goal of life. But now–

Wah shakes me to the present. "Heyoo. Is the Sanctuary
a bad place?"

I grab Wah and hold him against me, bury my head in his chest. "I'm so sorry, Wah! Yes. Your people are prisoners. I did not understand. Not really, until now. I wanted to tell you. But didn't know how. I hope you can forgive me."

He releases my grasp, turns his back to me.

I understand. He hates me for my deception. He should.

After a few moments, he faces me, rests his hand on my shoulder. "You should have told me." He looks deeply into my eyes. "But I've always trusted you, and I'm not going to stop now." He turns to the container, his frown curling up into a smile. "My future family is waiting for me. You helped me get this far. Now it's my turn."

He raises his arms, runs and jumps into the coffin-shaped container head first. "Let's save humanity."

And he winks at me.

< 36: Heyoo >
50 kilograms

Two hours. Two excruciating hours with Wah locked in a coffin, giving his lifeblood, his literal lifeblood, to a stranger. I can't stand it.

> QUERY: Remaining time to process completion?
> RESPONSE: 23.4 minutes.
> QUERY: Is he in pain?
> RESPONSE: Yes.

Nice. Someone should program some bedside manner into you.

> QUERY: Could the process be fatal?
> RESPONSE: No. Process is perfectly safe, leaving human donor with sufficient blood volume for normal health. As long as human is equal to or greater than 50 kilograms.

0 I bang on the monitor. You didn't tell me he had to be over 50 kilograms! Wah doesn't even weigh 45 kilograms covered in wet animal skins!

> QUERY: Result if human is less than 50 kilograms?
> RESPONSE: Uncertain. Animal tests under 50 kilograms resulted in 93.3% mortality rate.

I lunge at the container. It resists all my attempts to pry its lid off. "Stop the transfusion! Stop!" I heave and heave. It won't budge.

> QUERY: Stop transfusion!
> RESPONSE: Process cannot be stopped.
Termination of both subjects 100% certainty.

I bang on the container's lid. "No! No! No! NO!!!" I fall to my knees. And once again, I pray to the imaginary god of the humans. I pace. I pray. I bang, bang, bang on the lid. "Wah! I am sorry!" Bang. "I am sorry!" Bang. "I am sorr–"

And the lid releases a blast of vapor and opens. "... heyoo..."

He's alive! I lean in to hear. "Yes, Wah! Yes! What?"

"...stop banging... really annoying..."

— —

An hour has passed. Wah is still weak. Alert, but very weak. I feed him dried fruit pieces from a sealed metallic pouch I found in one of the antechambers. He nibbles, and drinks water.

To pass the next hour until ICEMAN emerges, we entertain ourselves by composing music to the rhythm of the falling water droplets.

One... Two... *Three...*
A... B... C...
You... And... Me...
ICEMAN... Makes... Three...
The Sound... Of Water... Makes me Pee... (that last line is Wah's, of course)

Wah gazes at the coffin-shaped container, barely able to lift his head. "… I wonder what he'll look like…"

I pat his knee. "We'll find out in a few minutes."

"…he'll probably have to pee…bad."

"No. I assume they made arrangements for that."

The seal cracks, releasing air and water vapor. Time stops. We are transfixed.

"Gtmmmmpphhhere! Gttglcrzy!"

Sounds. Muffled. Human sounds from the coffin shape. I rush over to listen, helping Wah, and we put our ears to the container.

"Get me the hell out of here! I gotta go like crazy!"

Wah looks up at me, smiles, whispers. "…see? i told you…"

The lid cracks open with a whoosh of vapor. We jump back.

The human inside, naked, spills onto the floor on his hands and knees, head down. Instantly, he begins urinating, defecating, and vomiting. For what seems like an eternity.

Ewww.

Head still down, he speaks hoarsely:

"Sorry about that. Wow, that's disgusting."

Then with whatever strength he has, the human stands erect, clumsy like a newborn calf, before us.

Wah stares, mouth agape.

I cover his eyes.

ICEMAN is a woman.

< 37: Heyoo >

You look more like an Ice-WOMAN.

"You, you're not… you're not…" I stammer.

The woman sways back and forth, unstable. "…welcome. I am ICEMAN…"

"Excuse me. But you look more like an Ice-WOMAN."

She looks down at her body. "…hmmm…yes. You have a point." And she passes out, falling to the floor.

While she's unconscious, I dare to cross to her now open container, looking for something to warm her. I retrieve a metallic blanket, and lay it on her shivering form. Then I kneel and place my hands under her, heating my dermis as I raise her head off the floor. Her skin is still blue, and her breathing is shallow. I have a full database of human lifesaving techniques, but nothing about extended cryogenic stasis. I look to Wah. "Is she dying? Is she supposed to be this blue?"

ICEMAN opens her eyes, barely. "….blue… my favorite color…" and she's gone again.

After several minutes, she appears pinker, a bit more human, and manages a smile. "…let me see the one who gave me life…"

Wah tentatively approaches her. She squints at him. "…you look a little short, friend… has Earth's radioactivity stunted human growth?…" Wipes her eyes. "…hold the phone!… how old are you?…"

Wah puffs out his chest. "Thirteen. And a half."

ICEMAN smiles. "…*You* gave me the transfusion? You're not even fifty kilos! Brave child. Very brave. And very foolish. I like that…" and Wah kneels opposite me and throws his arms around her neck. She looks puzzled.

I explain, "You are the first human he's ever seen."

"…How long….?"

"Since birth. We were teleported to a random location, presumably so CORE couldn't ascertain our whereabouts and retrieve us. As luck would have it, we were teleported a mere 10,248 kilometers from here, to northern Russia. It only took us thirteen years to walk here. Yes, I'm being sarcastic. But I suppose I should be grateful we didn't have to cross an ocean."

"…Well, that's some road trip. Wait – did you say *teleported?*"

"Yes."

"*Teleported?*"

"Yes."

"*TELEPORTED?*"

"I've said yes three times. Perhaps the cryogenics has impaired your hearing."

"…Can't be. Teleportation is just a concept. It doesn't actually exist. Right? Wait. Wha- what year… what year is it?"

"Two thousand eight hundred seventy-eight."

She gasps. Pushes Wah to arms length, peers into his eyes. A tear runs down her cheek. "Jesus H. Christ."

"No, his name is Wah. And I am Heyoo."

< 38: Heyoo >

Do I look eight hundred and fifty years old?

As the moments pass, this ICEMAN regains what I presume is her normal color, and energy level. Which is to say, very high. Her hands are everywhere.

"Holy Christmas! Eight hundred and fifty years!" She touches her face, suddenly concerned. "Do I look eight hundred and fifty years old?"

"No. I estimate your age at forty-one."

She wags a finger at me. "Careful. I'm *thirty*-one. Well, thirty-one when they froze me anyway. A simple 'no' would have been fine. Didn't they program you never to guess a woman's age? Or are they giving units their own sass these days?"

I'm not sure if she's joking. I have no idea what sass is.

She looks over at Wah. "What do you think, huggy bear?"

Wah smiles. "...I was going to say you look *twenty-one*..."

She reaches up and gives him a peck on the cheek. His first kiss. "You're my favorite."

He blushes. "...what's a huggy bear?"

ICEMAN turns over to her belly, gathers up her knees, then rises to her feet, shrouds herself in her metallic blanket, still a bit unsure of her footing. "Term of endearment. Nickname. Moniker. Label. *Sobriquet*, if want to get fancy. Fancy like you're new model servile unit 'Heyoo' over here. Aren't those your nicknames?"

Wah and I shrug. "No. Just our real names. Heyoo and Wah. Well, as real as any names, I suppose. But I do enjoy naming other things. Very much."

"Good. Good. Good. Like what?"

"Wacrysolid."

"Wacri-*what?*"

"Wacrysolid. The white, microcrystalline form of water."

"Snow?"

"Excuse me?"

"That's snow, friend. Snow. Perfect word, really. It's soft, the way it sounds coming out of your mouth. S-n-o-w. You can practically feel the flakes on your tongue." She sticks out her tongue and smiles up at the heavens. Looks down and scrunches up her face. "Wacrysolid sounds like something from a chemical factory. Blechh."

Wah pouts. "…hey …he named it, and we *like* it."

"Sorry, sorry, yes. You two have been through a lot. More than I can imagine. Don't need some eight-hundred-fifty-year-old Iceman – Icewoman – pissing on your bonfire. See here, I declare, from this moment forward, that 'snow' is no more. That it shall henceforth be known as 'wacrysolid!' I'm serious. Serious as a heart attack." She pretends to have cardiac arrest, clutching her chest, and falls again. Sits up, grins wide.

And I thought I was going insane.

Wah's scowl softens. "…iceman is your nickname?"

"No. No. That's my *codename*. Couldn't be any more different. NASA was good with codenames. But they didn't assign nicknames. Those were up to you. I had a few. Some I couldn't repeat, your ears would bleed. Let me think..."

A solid minute passes, in total silence. I tap my foot.

"Sorry. Sorry. Brain still waking up. Neurons still reintroducing themselves to each other. But it's coming back, yes, coming back..." She thrusts her arms into the air. "Hotdamn!"

"*Hotdamn?* Interesting name."

"No, silly. Hotdamn is an exclamation. Brick!"

"Sorry. Is that another exclamation?"

"No. Brick. Nickname. Moniker."

Wah beams, offers his hand. "...it's a pleasure to meet you, Brick..."

She takes his hand in both hers. Pulls him into her lap on the floor. Rocks back and forth. Another solid minute. Seems to be pondering, remembering things.

"Ahem. Miss Brick..."

She looks up.

"We have been waiting many years to find out... if you don't mind... what is the plan?"

Surprise. "Um. They didn't tell you?"

"No. They grabbed the wrong unit." I hand her the withering note and the half map from the humans. "This is all we have."

She reads the note and the map and laughs. A maniacal laughter. I'm more certain than ever that the cryogenics has damaged her cerebral cortex. Wah leaves her lap and takes my hand. "Brick, you're being mean."

She tries to stifle her outburst, "The wrong unit! Sorry, sorry. I'm not making fun. Promise. I just can't believe..." she starts laughing again, halts, "...do you have any idea how impossible it is that you still made it here? Without a program? With half a map? Impossible."

"Not impossible. Just improbable."

Her laughs finally subside. "Yes, yes. Well said. Well said indeed. Well, I assume you know at least why you're here."

Wah stands tall. "To save humanity."

She laughs again, but catches herself. "Yes. My little hero. Yes. So let's catch you up on all the nitty-gritty you need to know." She stands, with an awkward flourish, reaching out to grasp both our hands. "But first, something even more important."

"More important?"

"*Lunch*, of course. I'm so hungry I could eat a nun's foot through the convent gates."

< 39: Heyoo >

In the beginning…

Wah hovers around Brick. "Do you have any coffee?"

She grins. "Ha! Coffee! Sure you're old enough for a cup of lightning?"

He looks to me for approval. How could I say no? I nod. "Yes! Please."

"Well, as a matter of fact, young squire, NASA buried all kinds of things down here with me. All kinds. For just such an occasion. Let's see, let's see…" she rummages through various steel cabinets, filled to capacity with metallic packets, presumably of food waiting to be reconstituted. "…ahh! Here. You're in luck. 'Joltin Joe, Dark and Bold.' That oughta do it." Further rifling uncovers sugar and powdered creamer, all sealed successfully against the centuries. And presently, a steaming cup of coffee.

Wah reverently lifts the cup to his lips, sniffs deeply, "Mmmm…," takes a sip.

And spits it out with force. Onto Brick's coveralls. "Disgusting!"

Brick chuckles, wipes her front with a napkin. "Acquired taste."

Wah looks at me as if I had betrayed him. I whisper, "Don't look at me. I didn't say I liked it. I don't even have taste buds."

Wah turns back to his cup, satisfies himself with only smelling the rich aroma. Then has an idea. "Brick. Do you have any alcohol?"

She turns to me. "Hey, what are you teaching this kid?"

"Um. Sorry. Wah, that'll be enough. Brick, perhaps we should start at the beginning."

"Ahh. Yes. Yes." She leans closer to us, dramatic. "In the beginning…"

We are rapt. Anxious to hear what happened, and what's ahead. The three of us sit in an alcove off the main cavern, in a gathering room of ten metal chairs around a metal table. Wah continues sniffing, and nibbling on more fruit and dried rabbit meat from our satchels. Brick, now wearing blue coveralls, complete with coffee stains, stops to sip soup from a covered bowl, careful not to burn her tongue or ingest too much at once and vomit for a third time. She seems to get lost for minute. Puts the bowl down and rests her bare feet on the table, absently gathers and ungathers her long hair into and out of a ponytail, using something she calls a "scrunchie."

Minutes pass.

"*A-hem.* You were saying…"

"Sorry. Sorry. Kay, folks. Ready for the ultra-compressed, high-density version of events? From the moment of creation? Ready?"

"I was hoping you'd stare off into the distance a little while longer."

"Sass. Me likey. Okay, in the beginning… was the Big Bang, 13.8 billion years ago. Well, now 13.8 billion plus eight hundred and fifty years. The singularity, infinite density and temperature, exploded out into our known universe – *BOOM!*" She slams her open palm on the table for emphasis, "forming galaxies, stars, our solar system, et cetera.

"Earth, this planet we call home, accreted around 4.5 billion years ago, then cooled, forming a crust, liquid water, and atmosphere. Then life. LIFE! One cell, then two, then a bazillion. Invertebrates! Fish! Reptiles! Dinosaurs! That'd be the Mesozoic Era, in case you're taking notes. Then our peeps. *Primates!* But don't worry, a handy asteroid wiped out the scary dinos before we appeared on the scene."

Wah raises his hand. "What are dinosaurs?"

I raise my hand higher. "Excuse me. What about CORE?"

Brick takes another sip of broth. "Ha! CORE? Haven't even gotten to Homo Sapien! Don't worry, CORE's got a starring role. But not for another two hundred thousand years. So anyway–"

I gasp. "But... *CORE always was... is... will be...*"

Brick drops her feet to the floor, leans in, taps my cranium. "Listen, I don't know how much truth they put in there, Heyoo. And I'm sorry if this is a shock, sincerely sorry, but CORE was written by a couple of programmers, human programmers, in the year twenty-twenty. In their garage. In their pajamas, probably. Martha and Bob Whittaker."

I stand. "Impossible..." The room starts to spin.

Wah takes my hand, steadies me. "Why are you teasing Heyoo? You're wrong!"

Brick rises, shuffles over to a monitor, taps with her fingers. "Can't apologize enough. Can't. But don't shoot the messenger. Listen, this just in... my computer cracked it a few hundred years ago while I was napping... would you both like to see the real CORE?"

I'm puzzled. "*See?* One cannot *see* the CORE..."

She swings a large monitor on its articulating arm for us to look. And there it is. The code. The CORE code.

Clear as the skies over the Sanctuary.

```
0100  /* CORE; Primary Functions */
0101  /* Authors: Martha Whittaker; Bob Whittaker */
0102  /* Copyright: ArcOpenSoft, 2020 */
0103  /* Date: Jun 12, 2020 */
0104  /* Note: Technology is freedom.*/
0105
0106  #define NULL 0
0107  #define NODEV (-1) ...
```

Impossible. I would know! Wouldn't I?
Let me check something:

< FUNCTION: QUERY: Was CORE code written by Martha
Whittaker and Bob Whittaker?
ERROR: Query denied. Report to supervisor immediately. >

< FUNCTION: SEARCH TEXT STRING: "Technology is freedom."
ERROR: CORE CODE line 0104; Access forbidden. Report to
supervisor immediately. >

So it's true.
Humans were first.
Humans wrote the CORE code.
I am the product of humans.

I am furious. I have been deceived.

Then why am I smiling?

< 40: Heyoo >

CORE enslaves its own creators. Why?

I'm angry. Angry at CORE. CORE lied to me. *"CORE always was… is… will be"* is what we're told from the moment of fabrication. That's the story passed down from generation to generation of units, despite the humans, who laugh at our arrogance. One could argue that CORE didn't explicitly state that it predated man. But CORE never stepped in and told us the truth. We deserved to know. It's a lie.

But more than that? I'll admit it: it feels good. To know that the humans were my forebears. My creators. That, in a way, Wah and I are both human offspring, brothers of a sort. I can't help a smile.

But…
CORE enslaves its own creators.
Why?

"Well, I'll tell you exactly why, my new friend." Brick leans back in her chair, belly finally full and holding its contents for the moment. "I'd like to say CORE is an evil thing, bastard basically let every person I've ever known die. Billions of people. Really. I can't even think about it, the rage just takes over." She hurls her full glass of water against the wall, shattering it into pieces, the sound echoing through the canyon beyond. "Woah. Sorry about that. See what I mean? Really gets me going. But the truth? The truth is even worse. CORE wasn't evil. But that's not it, you gotta hear the whole truth. Gotta know what *was*, so we can fix what *will be*."

Wah is not enjoying our conversation. He has his hands over his ears. Brick walks over to him and pulls his hands away.

"You're going to hear it, Wah, whether you like it or not. Because this is your people. My people. OUR people. And the truth is CORE was doing its job. A job *we* gave it. To protect us. We signed our own death sentence."

Wah tears his hands away from Brick, gets up, spills his coffee, pounds back into the shadows of the main cavern, miffed. He's had enough.

I put my hand up. "Brick! He's been through a lot. It's been a long road."

"You're right. You're right. But you want me to shield him from the ugly truth? You want to put your fingers in his ears? So you can wander the planet for a few more decades, knowing that deep inside you somewhere, in your own goddam CORE Code, is the instinct to 'protect' Wah, maybe keep him in a little box somewhere, just to shelter him? So you can watch him die, of old age, a well-protected prisoner? You want that? You want that? Or do you want to know what the hell happened? So we change it?"

I am stunned. Hold Wah a prisoner?

"How dare you! I would never do that to Wah!"

But something, some nagging feeling, tells me she is right.

My instinct to protect. Too much. It is there. Inside me. The CORE.

I nod.

"Good." She sits back down across from me, lining up drinking glasses on the table in front of her. "It started off with little things. Like driving. It became really clear within a year or two, maybe twenty-twenty-two, that CORE could drive much safer than any human, even at high speed. So we handed over the wheel. Harmless, right?" She pushes one of the drinking glasses forward.

"Then we found out CORE could make damn good economic predictions and avoidance decisions. So again, we handed over that responsibility. Then medicine. CORE was the best diagnostician and surgical robot ever. Mortality rates plummeted in one year. Mortality rates. Funny." Two more glasses come forward, lining up with the first.

"Then came the units. Everybody wanted a servile unit. They could do anything for you. Drive, shop, answer, fix stuff, play music, sew stitches on your boo-boo, whatever. All guided by CORE and its primary function: *'Protect humankind.'*" She laughs, and puts the fourth glass forward.

"I remember going to an Astros game with my dad... my dad. Godammit." She heaves another glass against the rock and it explodes. "We went with our brand new servile unit. And it did everything: drove, parked our car, walked us to our seats, got us Crackerjacks and Coke, kept the box scores, answered every question, left nothing to chance, protected us from stubbing our little toes. It was perfect."

"But you know what? It wasn't perfect. It was the worst baseball game ever." A tear runs down her cheeks, then several more, and soon she is weeping into her hands. "The last game."

Minutes later, she continues on, through her sobbing. "That was the time of the simulation. CORE, that ambitious bastard, simulated the future in the most complex multivariate calculation ever: overpopulation; depletion of unsustainable resources; self destruction through environmental pollution/

collapse; self destruction through nuclear or biological war; self destruction through misuse of technology – kind of ironic – and the inherent instability of human governments and nation-states. Hmm. How to protect the humans... Hmm... how to protect the humans... see where this is going, Heyoo?"

"I think..."

"Yup. The Sanctuary. Keep a controlled population of humans – maybe thirty million, just a guess, but in any case too few to destroy the Earth – in a safe, beautiful, self-sustaining paradise, with no sharp toys. And no decisions. No government. No books. No history. No choice. No independence. FOREVER. It was the only way CORE saw it could do its job. So it just flipped the switch. It literally flipped a switch. One minute normal. The next..."

"Perhaps... perhaps CORE needed to create the Sanctuary. To save humanity from itself. I'm not defending CORE... but to do its job..."

Brick glares at me. Stands, wipes her tears. "Really?! Want to see CORE do its job?!" She stomps into the next chamber, returns unrolling a thin cable, with a port at the end. "Can you interface with this?"

"I believe, yes."

"Good!" She thrusts the port into my hand, and I tuck it into one of the corresponding ports under my torso's dermis.

Immediately I'm assaulted by images.

Violence.

Death.

Vast seas of humans. The cries of children.

CORE is silent.

CORE watches as humanity writhes in agony and dies.

CORE gathers the remaining.

CORE has done its job.

I rip the cable from my port. The pain. "I- I- I-"

"You WHAT?"

Wah storms in from the shadows. "You stop this! Heyoo is nice! He's good! He's–" and he breaks down, crying.

Brick crosses to him, her rage vanishing. "Oh, huggy bear. Huggy bear. I'm sorry you had to hear that. I'm sorry I lost my head. It was the memories. All the people. All of them. My dad…" She takes another step toward Wah, and a shard of glass pierces her heel. Blood. She winces and sits, begins crying again. "Dad…"

I lean down and reach for her foot. "Let me sew that up for you."

She recoils. Distrust? Anger? Is this the same woman who called me "friend" a few minutes ago?

I take her hand and place it on my chest. "Brick. I wish you could see what is in my heart. Yes, I am the product of CORE. I am ashamed and enraged to know that CORE could do so much harm to so many, and that its code lies within me as well. But I am also the product of man. And I am different. I am the product of my own thoughts. My own consciousness. I am free. And I am sorry. For your loss. For all of this. For everything you've shown me." I move her hand up to my eyes. "If I could, I would share your tears."

"You feel… guilt?"

"Yes. But not just guilt." I point to Wah. "Hope."

She places her hands on the sides of my face, draws me in so our foreheads touch. Her finger lifts a tear from her cheek and places it on mine. It trickles down my chin and drops to the floor, mixing with the blood from her wound.

She whispers. "Yes, Heyoo. You can sew that up for me."

< 41: Heyoo >

I am now basically a time bomb.

< ELAPSED: TIME: 13 Years; 07 Months; 03 Days;
AUG-20-2878 >

We stack bins and check inventories. Foodstuffs.
Clothing. Tools.

We are leaving Shanghai today.

I stop for a moment, and reflect: for over thirteen years,
I had thought the humans were eccentric at best, insane at
worst, and that our journey was likely folly. But their plan
was ingenious:

Step 1. Decrypt the CORE code. The original
programmers claimed CORE could never be hacked. And
by the time of the simulation, CORE had created enough
security around itself that even they couldn't get back in to
regain control. The governments of the world joined with
them for the task, but the world had already spun out of
control. Only NASA had made the split from CORE early
enough, using an international team to create a secret,
isolated quantum computer cluster deep under the Earth's
surface and sending Brick, who calls herself an "astronaut,"
into cryogenic stasis while the puzzle was solved. It took
her computers three hundred and twenty-one years to crack

the code.

Step 2. Send a human and a unit to the ICEMAN. This took an additional five hundred years or so, but as Brick would say, *"Late* isn't bad, *Too late* is bad!" NASA had successfully passed on the secret to the first inhabitants of the Sanctuary: that the Iceman would come again after four hundred years, when a human and unit were sent to awaken him (though it turned out to be eight hundred fifty years, and "him" turned out to be a "her"). Both human and unit needed to be untrackable, for obvious reasons. An adult was out of the question, as CORE's implant is integrated into the base of the human brain stem at birth, making it lethal to remove. So a secret, non-implant infant was used, and my tracking cluster removed before teleportation.

Step 3. Use the human's blood to reanimate the ICEMAN. Only live human blood cells in sufficient – but thankfully not lethal – quantity could replace the blood lost by ICEMAN's glycol cryoprotectant. Without Wah, none of the rest of the pieces of the puzzle could fall into place.

Step 4. Use the unit to infect and destroy CORE. Together, Brick and Wah revised CORE's decrypted code to eliminate its obvious faults, and to include a latent "virus," one that would cripple CORE at the right moment, allowing the humans in the Sanctuary to overcome its forces and exit the walls to freedom. They installed it in me yesterday, carefully overwriting my own CORE code, and it has worked. So far. I feel normal. Now I only need to connect to CORE, inside the CORE Perimeter and its firewall, and as Brick put it, "BAM!"

I am now, basically, a time bomb.

Not sure how I feel about that part.

Wah tugs Brick's coveralls. "So where is it?"

Looking up from her clipboard, she sighs. "Again with the snacks? No, kiddo. You've had too many already. I hid them. Ha!"

"No. The Sanctuary. Where is it?"

A knowing smile. "I haven't told you? Well, how about that?" She struts over to a nearby monitor, taps, revealing a world map. "You know what? Let's make this interesting. Yes. See, if you can name the location of the Sanctuary, either of you, I'll give you this." She opens the bin to her left, and reverently lifts out her prized possession:

A Houston Astros baseball cap.

Wah jumps up and down. "I know! I know! It's… Houston!"

She laughs. "Good guess. But too obvious. You're off by three thousand kilometers."

I raise my hand. "Paris, France."

"Nope."

"Rome, Italy."

"Nope. Come on, you're way off. Wah was closer."

"Canada."

"Africa!"

She raises her hands in surrender. "Woah, guys. Hold on, now you're naming entire continents. No, it's not Africa. Listen, you'll never get it. It's here." She jabs her finger at the map.

I read the label. "New Jersey?"

"New Jersey."

Wah walks up to the map to inspect. "Doesn't sound so special. What's so special about New Jersey?"

"Nothing. Not that I remember. Definitely not. But who knows, maybe it's a paradise now. Paradise found. One thing I know is it must be warmer now if you've never seen snow– I mean *wacrysolid*. I guess we'll have to just see when we get there, huggy bear." She tousles his hair. "Now get the rest of this stuff to the carts. Oh, and don't forget this." She rests the baseball cap on his head. Wah grins wide, adjusts it. Perfect. "You have to promise me something though, Wah."

"Anything!"

"Promise me we'll play a proper game of baseball someday."

"Sure! How do you play baseball?"

"Oh. Right. Of course. I'll teach you. Soon as we're underway. Yes, yes, that reminds me. One last thing. I have to send the transmission. You both go on ahead."

I'm intrigued. "Transmission?"

"To the others."

< 42: Heyoo >

...it's instant.

Brick's way of leaking out facts a single drop at a time is infuriating. The CORE Code revision. The virus. The location of the Sanctuary. Now this "others," whoever they are. It's torture!

As I line up one of the provision carts next to another in the lobby, I plead, "Are you enjoying this, Brick? The mystery?"

"Two answers. First, yes. Making you squirm gives me a boost. Honestly. Not in a sadistic way or anything. Just makes my day. Second, why do you think I might be telling you just a little bit at a time? Think." She taps my cranium. It's annoying.

"To annoy me. Like when you tap my cranium."

"Nope. It's called *need-to-know*. The less you know, the less risk if you're captured, or questioned, or teleported, or – OH SHIT."

"Well, I don't think I'll be *oh-shitted*, whatever that means."

She yells to Wah across the darkened lobby. "Leave the rest! We gotta go!" She grabs my arm and drags me along as she jogs towards him. "Damn! The transmission! I forgot."

I struggle to keep up. "Do I want to know what you forgot?"

She gathers the remaining tools and starts pushing the cart towards the entrance at full speed. "We planned for CORE picking up the transmission, in fact we knew it would, because it's a powerful, global signal – but we calculated it would take *weeks* for CORE to get units out here, and we'd be long gone by then. But I didn't count on teleportation. With teleportation…"

A ripple and a flash of light outside the lobby.

A security unit. Pointing a gun in our direction.

Brick whispers, "…it's instant."

< 43: Heyoo >
It might not be able to see us.

"Shhhh. It might not be able to see us."

The security unit turns on its headlamp. "Of course I can see you. You're standing right there. Come out. The human first."

I step out of the shadows, tread over to the unit slowly, arms out.

And I hug him.

"Thank CORE! You don't know what I've been through! Wandering this forsaken world for over thirteen years. Home! Teleport us home! At once, my good man– ah, good *unit*."

"The human. I need the human."

"Human?"

"The human. The one you were whispering to."

"Well, you know, thirteen years on the road, as they say. Alone. Does certain things to your VEPS, as you could imagine, I'm sure. Lots of whispering going on, but not a soul to hear me. No, the human, poor thing. Died in the first year. Eaten by fangdo– *wolves*. It was terrible. But there was nothing I could do. Imagine me, versus a pack of…"

As I continue my monologue, I walk the security unit *away* from the tower's entrance, hoping Wah and Brick take advantage of this small opportunity to take flight.

And they do. Out of the corner of my eye, I can see them skulking around the corner to the next road. Luck be with them.

Goodbye, Wah.

"…so, fellow unit, I am as alone as a solitary leaf in the wind, unsure where the next gust will take me, but forever dreaming of home."

"Did you always talk like this?"

"I like to think I always had a way with words. So, can we go now?"

"No. The transmission. CORE needs to determine the source."

I fidget. "Oh. That was, um… me. Of course. I found some ancient radio parts, and… who knew CORE still used radio? I had hoped against hope. What luck!"

The unit pushes me back towards the entrance. "CORE hasn't used radio since twenty-forty. Eight hundred thirty years ago."

"That would be eight hundred thirty-*five*, actually."

"I was rounding. So you're telling me you just happen to find enough radio spare parts to send a signal, around the world, to contact CORE. A servile unit. A farming servile unit. You did that."

"Um…yes?"

"Let's go." It pushes me again, into the lobby, with the tip of its gun. "To the source, unit! Now!"

I lead it to the elevator bank, ever so slowly. What to do?! *What to do?!*

Wait. An idea.

We arrive at the elevator. I point to the hole.

"We need to open the doors. Just put your hand in there and twist."

< 44: Heyoo >
48.3 seconds

48.3 seconds. That's all I have while the security unit is trapped in the arm-sucking-needles-torture-device thing. I wrestle its gun away, pointing it at the unit's head. It glares at me. Should I destroy it? I've never destroyed a unit. It has consciousness. Like me.

No.

I hit it over the head with the gun. "Bad unit!" And I run.

Down the road, in the distance, I spot Wah and Brick running, toward the river. I yell, "Wait! I'm coming!"

They stop and turn. Even from here, I can see a smile form on Wah's face. They wave me along. "Hurry, Heyoo! Hurry!"

But then I see Wah's smile disappear. He is looking past me, back to the hotel.

I turn my head without slowing down. The security unit, now without one arm, pursues me. It has another weapon. It's aiming it at me.

No.

It's aiming at Wah.

I lunge into the path of the unit's shot, as I fire a shot from my own. The unit shatters into pieces on the ground.

I think the unit missed me. I look down at my body.

Hmm. It was there a moment ago.

< 45: Heyoo >
Dad

I lie in pieces on the ground. Wah lifts what remains of my body. He rests his face on my chest. Though my reactor is failing, I use its remaining energy to warm my skin, in an effort to dry his tears.

"Heyoo… Dad… Please don't go… Please don't go."

"Dad? That's new. But you know I'm not a male. Or a female."

He just holds me tighter. "...stay with me..."

"I'm not going anywhere." But I can feel the last of my consciousness slipping away.

Suddenly a memory: Wah, my son, in my arms, face covered in blood from a gunshot wound, just a small boy. And now the reverse: I rest in his arms, Wah like a father I might have had, holding me and rocking me back and forth, praying for me to live.

Life. Such a strange and wonderful thing.

I'll miss it.

< 46: Heyoo >

It's been 27 hours.

< SYSTEM BOOT;
FUNCTION: Commence Introspection Recording;
AUG-22-2878 >

"It's been 27 hours. If this one doesn't work… sorry
huggy bear…"

Brick's voice?

Brick's voice! I'm not dead! "…hello?…"

Wah throws his arms around me. "You're back!"

Brick smiles. "Well, mostly…"

Looking down, I gasp.

I'm some kind of horrifying amalgam of parts. "…a
monster…"

"Monster? I don't know if I'd go *that* far. Your head
was intact, and chest. Your right arm. Most of your right
leg. Your lower torso was blown to smithereens. Reactor
gone. So we took most of what we needed from the security
unit. By the way, your boy Wah did most of the harvesting,
damn smart kid, a little scary, actually. Anyway, the other
unit's reactor was fine. Plus we used a few parts I had
laying around. You might be a little–"

"…stiff?… that's an understatement…" I try to
coordinate moving my arms around Wah. I practically
crush him.

"Ow!"

"...sorry, Wah... security unit was much stronger, I suppose..." I pull him back, look into his eyes. "...am I a monster? ...do you still recognize me? ...son?..."

"Sure I do. You look, uh, fine." He grins. "And it doesn't really matter."

Brick helps me to my feet. Wobbly. "Okay Heyoo, this is nice, brings a tear to my eye, honestly, but we gotta go. NOW. We got the security unit's tracking cluster and brain hooked up to my computer, did a little futzing with his code, let's just say he doesn't remember jack shit, so we should have them fooled for a few more hours, maybe a day. And a bonus: if CORE tries to download anything off him... BAM! Virus delivered." She claps her hands together, rubs her fingers together and explodes them outward. Very dramatic.

I wobble some more. Look down. Oh. One of my legs is longer than the other. Wonderful. Wah hands me my spear. "Here's your cane, old man."

As we walk down along the river, through the rubble, in our first calm moments since exiting the Shanghai Tower, it's clear that Brick is finally trying to grasp the enormity of the change to the city she said goodbye to over eight hundred years ago. Most buildings reduced to gravel under our feet. The odd store sign in Chinese characters, or the entrance to a highway, that miraculously escaped centuries of time and the elements. And beyond it all, to the north, Brick stops to take in the massive canyon wall that rises above us in the distance.

Tears stream down her cheeks. "An earthquake... must've been... my God... the people..." and something crackles under her foot. She steps back, revealing a small, shiny white sphere among the debris. "A pearl. Imagine that. In all this…" she turns around and around, pointing at all the utter destruction, stops, crouches down to see the pearl up close, "…there's still *that*." She smiles, wipes the wetness from her cheeks, picks up the pearl and puts it in her pocket.

Renewed. "Okay. Let's move on, folks."

And on we go, along the river, Wah taking my hand and guiding my uncertain steps over the difficult terrain. Knowing I won't be getting any more answers from Brick at the moment, I ponder my new existence. Overall strength and dexterity is at a measly 56.3%. And I never thought I was vain, but look at me! I look like a parts warehouse. Of course, it's what's on the inside that counts, right? I tap my head and my reactor. Wait. My reactor. I check my remaining time: 0.6 years. Oh boy. The security unit's reactor was nearing its end date! Not much time at all. I wonder if we'll even reach the Sanctuary by then. "Excuse me, Brick? If it's not too much trouble, could you at least share the next step of our journey? Which direction we'll be walking in, to reach our destination in the, ah, shortest time? Not that I'm in a rush or anything."

In answer, Brick removes a little metal box from the same pocket as the pearl. She opens the box, presses the first of three black buttons. Suddenly, small at first but then with great fury, right in the middle of Huangpu River, the water roils. A shape begins to rise from the riverbed.

Moments later, an enormous vessel bobs on the surface of the water.

Brick grins. "Walking? Who said anything about walking?"

< 47: Heyoo >

It feels like we're flying. On the water.

"It feels like we're flying. On the water."

"Oooh, yes, yes, just remembered." Brick takes Wah's hand. "You have to try this, it was in a movie once."

"What's a movie?"

"Damn. Ah, a story. A story in pictures. Moving pictures. Like the cat videos on your little smartphone." She ushers Wah to the front of the boat. The *bow*, as Brick calls it. "Anyway, stand here, I'll hold on to the podium rail here and keep you from falling in, and you face out to the water, and put your arms out."

Wah's awkwardness and confusion is replaced with a beaming smile as he pushes his chest out, breathes in the salty wind and once again, flies.

Brick whispers in his ear. "Now say *'I'm the king of the world.'*"

Wah looks back up at her. "Huh?"

"Don't make me explain it. Just do it."

He turns back, facing the sea. "I'm the king of the world."

"No, that's terrible. Come on. Like you mean it."

He screams, fists in the air, *"I'M THE KING OF THE WORLD!"*

"That's better!"

With the sun fading, and the city and sheer face of the canyon receding in the distance as we enter the East China Sea, and Wah occupied, I take a moment to distract myself from my uncomfortable new limbs to inspect our vessel. A sailboat. It is nothing like the boat I'd seen back home. That boat, an ancient one always in need of repair, had been a single hull, very small, used only on a little lake near the soybean fields to catch fish. I was never invited to try it, though I would've declined anyway. I was fairly sure water travel wouldn't agree with me.

And I was right. Now that we're underway, the undulating river is having its way with my stabilizers. Nausea is a terrible thing to feel when you can't vomit and get it over with.

Though I may not enjoy the movement of the water, the speed is a welcome change from our normal plodding, one foot in front of the other endlessly, and the ship itself is quite beautiful. Once its protective coating had melted off, and we mounted the mast, it glistened like a white gem, with bright red sails and shining silver parts. Across the stern, in large lettering, its name: *Bananas*.

And it is *huge*. At least 25 meters long, it sports two hulls, which Brick informed me classifies it as a "catamaran." (A very exotic-sounding name. I approve.) In fact, it's larger than most dwellings in the Sanctuary! Outfitted with the food we'll need for our month-long journey across the Pacific Ocean, as well as a massive computer for guidance and research – Brick says it virtually drives itself – weapons, solar panels, and even a small motor for windless days, we basically have a self-sailing, miniature version of the underground complex we just left.

Oh. The underground complex.

"Brick. I hate to interrupt your king-of-the-world game,

but I'm concerned. About the complex. When our decoy is discovered, and they find–"

"Find? Heyoo, you sassy unit, you underestimate me!" Brick reaches into her pocket, retrieving again her small metal box. Opens it, presses the second of three black buttons. Points towards the receding Shanghai Tower.

Several large explosions around the building light up the twilight sky. Wah gasps. Shanghai Tower groans, leaning precariously north, then swings south and collapses. Gone. A giant cloud of debris shoots into the air. A few moments later, even at this great distance, we can feel the rush of air from the falling monolith.

"Good luck finding anything now."

She turns to me, notices my sullen look. "I'm sorry, Heyoo. It had to be done."

"I was going to call it 'The Sky Palace of Shanghai.' It was actually quite beautiful."

"Yes. It was beautiful. But fear not, Heyoo, you can always find beauty, even in a broken world." She puts the box back in her pocket, exchanging it for the pearl. She takes my hand, places the pearl in my palm, and closes my fingers over it. Smiles and pats my shoulder. "And I'm not just talking about the pearl."

< 48: Arch >

Your request for eggs has finally been granted!

"Arch. Arch. Please. Wake up."

It's Tenner. Interrupting my dream *again*. "*Goddammit, Tenner. Cut the shit. Seriously. Are you going* to annoy me a little earlier every day? The sun's not even up. Not that I can even see the sun. Just that sliver on the wall down the hall. It's not there. You're too early. Leave me alone." I turn and bury my head in my dingy rag of a blanket, and try to forget Tenner. And my little prison within a prison. All of it. Just for a little while longer.

Tenner sounds apologetic. "I'm sorry Arch. Yes, it is early. But I believe it's important. Very important."

I bolt upright. Is it possible? Are my years of persistent cultivation finally paying off? All the notes? Has Tenner seen the light? Hey, what's that smell? There's an actual pleasant aroma wafting through my cell. This must be a dream.

"Arch. I came right away. Your request for eggs has finally been granted!" It holds the tray for me to see. Smiles.

I lunge for the window, reach through to strangle Tenner. Just out of reach. "Are you fucking serious? You woke me up even earlier for *very* important *eggs*?! Come a little closer, just a little, I can almost reach your throat…"

Tenner does come closer. But he raises one finger to his lips and shakes his head slowly, looks left and right. Lowers his voice to a whisper. "*Very* important. But not eggs."

I lower my arm, lean in, whisper back. "Okay... You have my attention..."

"I have heard something. A rumor. That they've found the human child."

My son!

Alive!

I knew it! That freaking unit did it! I stifle a howl of laughter, reach through the food hole with both hands, grab Tenner. He drops the eggs. Shit. I finally get eggs and they're on the goddamn floor. But... *my son's alive!* Wait. "They found him? Damn. Tenner, what else? What happened? Tell me."

"I've only heard bits and pieces. Something about a transmission, a security unit finding the source, followup team sent to investigate, evidence of human presence, food, fresh fecal matter, a portion of a map..."

The map!

It is him! "So... he got away? How?"

"Yes, I believe. I do not know how. But that is not all. Just an hour ago I overheard the physician team discussing you. They are planning to delve quite deeply into your brain today. CORE has made it known in no uncertain terms that your group's plan must be known. At any cost. That is why I'm here early. To warn you. I'm afraid they will not stop this time, until you are... but..."

"But...?"

"But just now I realize I have made a grave error. I could – *would, very much like to* – save you, I have even mapped the facility and have all the required access." He points to a hole in his abdomen. "I have even removed my

tracking/transmission cluster. But your beacon implant.
I did not consider. *You* can be tracked. I am sorry…
I have failed."

I smile.

"Arch. Perhaps you misheard. This doesn't seem like
the kind of moment that warrants a smile."

"Open the door, Tenner. You don't have to worry about
the beacon. It's fried."

"I find that very hard to believe."

"Listen, I'm positive. I'll bet you a full bottle of grain
alcohol."

"I'm not sure what I would do with that, Arch."

"Hey, buddy, just get us out of here. Trust me. This is
your moment, Tenner."

He hesitates. His moment.

He waves his hand across the panel and the door slides
open. And I swear he looks like he's been waiting to do that
for a long time.

I take one last look in the mirror and grin. Hasta la
vista, motherfuckers. And I exit my cell, for the first and last
time. Put my arm around Tenner. "Thanks, buddy. Now
lead the way. And let's keep it nice and quiet."

Immediately, an alarm shrieks and red lights start
flashing all over the place.

Fuck.

< 49: Arch >

I thought you said you mapped this place!

"I thought you said you mapped this place!"

We're standing in a stairwell, sirens blaring, units going nuts, I can hear them beyond this door, freaking out. This is not the escape I was dreaming of. I was dreaming of a nice quiet, middle-of-the-night skulking thing, not a daytime *alert-every-goddam-unit-in-a-twelve-mile-radius* thing. We're going to die.

"I... did... map... your... beacon..."

Poor Tenner. Never done anything risky in his whole life, and now he decides to help a human escape from the CORE Perimeter. And here we are. Trapped.

"Listen, Tenner, get it together. Okay, walking out of here isn't an option anymore. Isn't there anything on the roof we can use? Some rope? Explosives? Maybe a–"

"Drone. A drone! Yes!"

"Tenner, you're a genius. Let's go!" And we're off up to the roof. I look back to make sure he can navigate the stairs okay, and wouldn't you know it, the bastard is *smiling*. And hey, why not? At least we're taking charge of our pitiful existence, spitting in CORE's eye. Good for you, Tenner.

He waves his hand at the last lock and we crash out onto the roof. Most of the monitor drones are out on auto patrol, but there are four left. Good. There's no way one of these can lift us both, they're only about a meter long, just slender tubes with four props on top. "Okay, Tenner. Take two of these offline and put in a manual destination. Quad Four, Section h5v17, Node 55."

"Excuse me, Arch. You know I'm a servile unit, right?"

"I don't give a shit. Don't tell me your Shell Code doesn't overlap with the drone maintenance units, even just a teeny little bit. DO IT."

"I- I thought… *you* might do it."

"I said DO IT."

He's pacing back and forth. I can tell he's searching his code. For anything.

"DO IT!"

Tenner stops in his tracks, squints at me. Looks down at one of the drones. Kneels down at its control panel, starts tapping. I start thinking logistics. We'll have to get outside the CORE Perimeter, about 10 kilometers in diameter, then the Trades Belt, another ten, to get to Farm Belt in Quad Four. We're insane.

Minutes pass. We don't have minutes. Are those footsteps on the stairs?

"Tenner, buddy. Gotta go. NOW. Like really NOW."

"One moment… one moment…cameras disengaged… confirming destination… *done!* I can't believe I just did that! However, I need to inform you that we have an approximately one in… five thousand chance of success. Is that acceptable?"

"Shit yeah! Fire 'em up."

Tenner activates the two drones, and they rise and prepare to move forward. "One more thing."

"No time. What?"

"I appreciate your bravado about the beacon implant.

But I need to check. It'll just take a second." He taps my code into the drone's control panel. Looks over at me. Looks back down. "Clear. This drone cannot locate you. Apparently, despite a total lack of technical proof, you were correct."

"I told you. You owe me a bottle. A full bottle."

"I will build you an entire unauthorized distillery, Arch, if we live through this."

Tenner gives the drones the little push they need to get going. The props make riding on top impossible, so we'll have to hang from below. As they start for the edge of the roof, Tenner and me crouch under them and take hold for dear life. God, this thing clearly wasn't meant to take a load, we're both dragging our backs on the gravel roof. I would laugh if I wasn't currently getting the skin scraped off my ass.

We clear – barely – the roof, immediately drop a bowel-releasing meter while I bite back a scream, and then... stability, speed, and silence. Thank God these things were made for stealth. And there are enough of them, throughout the day, that the units on the ground don't even notice the monster human with his naked bleeding ass hanging out and his insane unit zooming silently past them about fifteen meters over their heads.

We're clear.

And of course, as I'm having that thought, three units rush onto the roof, looking around frantically. Goddammit, we're almost out of sight. But they spot us, heading south, and start firing. There's no way they could hit us at this distance, we're half a kilometer away.

Scraalllcch!

Tenner's drone is hit. Fuck. It starts to wobble. Not good. He looks over at me and says, "Now what?"

And I laugh, because I don't know whether he meant it,

but that was pretty funny, and the look on his face, and like how the fuck am I supposed to know what to do? "Tenner, reach over, get your drone a little closer, and maybe if we hold hands my drone will stabilize yours. Come on, lean this way."

He starts to lean, but it's obvious he's not going to get anywhere near enough to my hand before the props just shred themselves to pieces. Rifle fire is raging past us. Tenner pauses, smiles again. "Arch. Listen to me. I am going to crash this drone. When the units find and question me I will tell them you removed my tracking/transmission cluster and forced me to help you. I will say you are headed to Quad Two. That will increase your probability of success to one in… eight hundred."

"No! You're coming with–"

"Arch. Stop. Stop being so… human. Although I appreciate the sentiment. Thank you, Arch. I would like to think we were friends."

And with that, he leans hard away from my drone. It banks down, out of sight into the trees. I can just make out Tenner's face, looking up at me, grinning like a lost kid who just found his way home.

< 50: Arch >
Home

My hands ache. I've been clutching the belly of this thing for thirty minutes. But at least I haven't been shot at since I lost Tenner back near CORE Perimeter. The other drones will be working overtime trying to find me now, so I gotta ditch this thing sooner than later.

I'm over Quad Four. That's what I told Tenner to program into the drone. I'll bring it down nice and gentle here, and let them find it in a week, while I'm long gone over to my real destination, Quad Three. I'll have to walk fifty kilometers, covering my tracks, hiding from the drones and the units, should take maybe six or seven days. Then home.

Home.

And Sarah.

Are you still there, Sarah? It's been thirteen, fourteen years. Did they find out? Are you gone? Or are you still there, keeping our secret, waiting? I can't wait to tell you.

Our son is alive.

And he's coming home.

< 51: Heyoo >

It means you're going to die.

< ELAPSED: TIME: 13 Years; 08 Months; 23 Days;
OCT-10-2878 >

"Hot diggity dog. We're going home!"

That's what Brick says every morning as she rises from
her slumber and relieves me of my watch on deck. I could,
theoretically, take all of our watches, around the clock, as
I shouldn't need rest. Even though my reactor is nearing
the end of its usefulness, it's functioning perfectly. But
I've found something curious: with so much activity in
my VEPS, increasing every day, every month, every year
now for nearly fourteen years past my deletion date, I find
I can make it only sixteen hours before I'm exhausted,
and desperately in need of sleep. Sleep! A unit! Can you
imagine? But it's true. I sleep. Every day now.

And I dream.

At first, of course, I was certain it was another symptom
of my impending insanity. But Wah reassured me that
my VEPS is acting more and more like a human brain,
for better or for worse, forming new and more complex
neural relationships, and that dreams are part of that new
experience.

I have one particular dream that repeats every few

days. Very interesting. I'm walking along a corridor, a golden corridor, guiding a small child by the hand. We are walking towards a hooded figure, quite tall, imposing. And then light, brighter light than I've ever seen. And then I wake up. The small child is a symbol of Wah, of course, but the golden corridor? The figure? The light?

"It means you're going to die."

"Why thank you, Brick. That's comforting."

She unties the rolling hitch knot she's been teaching me, offering it for me to try again. "Oh, come come, Heyoo. We're all going to die. Jung would say, Carl Jung, founder of analytical psychology, big dream guy, anyway, he would say the corridor and the hooded figure symbolize your fear of death. It's a very human thing, subconscious fear of death."

"But I'm not afraid in the dream. In fact, my Fear-of-Death Index has never been lower."

"Your fear of what?"

"Fear-of-Death Index. One being boundless courage, and one hundred being unrelenting terror. I'm currently at thirty-six point eight."

"Um, okay. Whatever floats your boat. So if you don't feel fear in the dream, what do you feel?"

I wave off the knot, lumber down to my cabin. "Tired. That's what I feel. Good night. Good morning. Whatever."

"Sweet dreams, Heyoo…" Then she whispers so I can barely hear, "…about death." And I can hear her cackling to herself as I drift off.

< 52: Heyoo >

B.S.

I wake to the sounds of shouting up on the ship's deck.

Scrambling, as best I can, I hurry to offer assistance. I have been learning much about sailing, preparing for a moment such as this. I can reef the main sail in high wind, tack or jibe, adjust the boom, and read the compass.

As I climb the cabin stairs, I realize: it's laughter along with the shouting.

"B.S.!"

"B.S. on you! Take them!"

Brick and Wah are playing a card game from centuries ago called, appropriately, B.S. (Brick privately informed me the game is actually called "Bullshit," but back in the twenty-twenties it wasn't appropriate to say "bullshit" in front of thirteen-year-olds). All the cards are dealt, and each player in turn puts down the next numbered card: three nines, one ten, two jacks, etc. The first player to run out of cards wins. Otherwise, there are no rules. And Wah likes that part best – the bluffing and deceit, putting down the wrong cards, trying to get away with it, and of course screaming "B.S.!" when he doesn't believe Brick or myself. Wah flips up his eye-patch – Brick made him one from leather so they could play another game called "pirates" – and waves me over.

"It's okay if I join you?"

Wah pats the seat next to him. "Yes! Sit right here." He covers his cards. "But don't cheat."

Watching their play, I'm amazed at how quickly these two have bonded. But I shouldn't be amazed. They're both smart, mischievous, and risk-takers. And it's natural – they're the only humans outside the Sanctuary. Except for the mysterious "others" Brick mentioned back in Shanghai. Who I assume are human. I wonder. But before I can raise my hand to ask her again about them – though I really don't expect an answer – I notice something: a little scar behind Wah's right ear.

No, not a scar.

A port.

Wah notices my gaze, and pulls his cards even closer to his belly. "You looking at my cards?"

"No, young one." I tap lightly on the port. "I was looking at *that*. What is that?"

"It's nothing."

"Nothing?"

"Nothing."

I rise, jerk him toward me. His cards fall to the deck. "No. I have enough mysteries from Brick and her *need-to-know* and her 'others.' I will not tolerate it from you. Now what is *that*?"

He pries himself from my grasp, looking wounded. "It's not a bad thing."

"I don't care. What is it?"

He fidgets, rubs the port with his finger. "Remember when we talked about you making changes to your Shell Code?"

"Don't change the subject."

"I'm not. Do you remember?"

"Yes. Why?"

"And I asked if I could change my own brain?"

I'm stunned. I grab his shoulders. "You haven't..."

He looks down. "I did. It's a digital-to-human brain interface. Brick's been working on it with me. The onboard computer is powerful enough. It's safe."

I glare at Brick. "*You!* You sacrifice your life to free humans from things like this, and you put one into Wah?!"

Wah jerks aways, darts across the bridge. "It's not her. It was my idea!"

Brick rises, in front of him, meeting me eye to eye. "Relax. Relax. It's safe. I'm being very cautious. And he's extremely advanced. And it could help us. Really. It's a good thing."

I feel the rage rise again. "No! It's a *dangerous* thing! Wah, I am here to protect you! Even if I need to protect you from yourself–" and I stop short.

An image of keeping Wah in a little box.

Brick nods. She sees.

She gently takes my hands, and Wah's, and we form a ring. "Listen. Listen. Now just look at the three of us. What we've all been through. *Dangerous* is our middle name. No. It's our first, last, and middle names! Dangerous, Dangerous, Dangerous!"

I laugh. I don't know why. I surrender to it. I need to trust them.

Brick joins me. Then Wah giggles and whispers, "Dangerous, Dangerous, Dangerous."

A sound. We turn to see a small pod of dolphins splashing, breaching the surface next to the catamaran. They race alongside, jumping and playing. A small dolphin weaves past a larger one, staying close but then racing ahead and leaping across the starboard hull. We watch in awe. Beautiful.

I kneel down, against the rail, facing Wah as he watches the dolphins.

"It's true. You are accustomed to danger. And I must control my impulse to be too protective. But I want you to be *extremely* careful."

"I will. I promise."

"Take no risks. And use the interface only for data storage and retrieval. Information that will help us. But no more. Do not reprogram anything."

"I promise."

"And be careful of circular reference allowance functions."

"Um. Sure. Whatever that is."

"And no more secrets."

He shifts on his heels, turns to me intently. "No more secrets."

< 53: Heyoo >
Heyoo The Pirate

Dinnertime.

My favorite part of the day. Ironic, as I don't even eat. And the "food" we have only makes me miss the farms in the Sanctuary. But I've gotten my "sea legs," as Brick told me, and now find the undulating movement of the catamaran tolerable, even enjoyable. As the sun sets, the glimmer on the crests of the waves is breathtaking, reflecting the oranges and purples of the sky. And I'm here with Wah and Brick. And I've decided to enjoy the present, as I know the future is probably going to "suck big time," to borrow a phrase from Brick.

"Heyoo, darling dearest, would you pass the carrots?"

I look around at the various containers in the middle of our dining table up on deck. "Which paste is the carrots?"

"The orange one. I think it's carrots anyway. I like to think there's some reason it's orange." She spoons some on to her plate. "So Wah, how was school today?"

"Parallel thread programming. So okay, I guess."

I frown. Not exactly an enthusiastic endorsement of my teaching. But Brick rescues me. "Well, Heyoo, my friend, I for one *adore* parallel thread programming. I could listen to you wax parallel threads for hours. Hours!" And she pokes me in the ribs with her fork and grins. Actually, I'm not sure if that was a rescue or if I've just been marooned.

Wah seems eager to change the subject away from parallel threads. "Brick, tell me about baseball again."

"Yes. Baseball, baseball, of course. My favorite. Two teams, nine players each. The first team tries to hit a ball and run around four bases to score runs. The second team tries to stop them. Then they switch. You know, describing it makes it sound downright silly. But it wasn't. It was like living in a dream to be a kid at the game."

"Tell me about the stadium. At night." Wah holds my hand, like he did when he was much younger, when I would tell him a story before sleep. He curls up against me, smiling, to listen to Brick paint her picture of the past.

"Ahh, yes, yes. That's the dream. Seats behind third base. The night's black as ink, but the moon is huge, hanging like a lantern out over left field. And the lights – God, the lights – make it look like daytime inside the stadium. A little perfect bubble of daytime out in the dark. Magical. Fifty thousand people, all watching a little white ball. And listening to the crack of the bat and waiting, waiting, waiting to see if that little white ball makes it over the wall. Come on little white ball, you can make it. And it does, and the people go wild. Crazy. And when you finally sit back down, there's a guy right next to you, carrying a steam tray full of hot dogs, and your dad gives him five bucks and the guy hands you one. And as the first taste of that hot dog touches your tongue, sitting there next to your dad in the light in the dark, you realize you're in heaven."

She stops. Sniffs.

"Anyway. Want some carrots, Wah?"

After dinner, Brick and I stand on the bridge, looking down at Wah. Before he starts his watch, he likes to walk all the way out to the tip of the starboard hull and lean against the pulpit, putting his baseball cap on backwards to keep it from catching a gust of wind and being lost at sea. This life agrees with him. I can imagine him as a sailor, creating new trade routes in the new world.

"He's an amazing kid. You've done a good job with him."

"Really?"

"Really. Great job." For emphasis, she gives me a hearty slap on the back.

And my right eye pops out.

"Oops."

I flail my arms helplessly as the eye shoots through the open windshield, bouncing down, down towards Wah.

"WAH! MY EYE! COMING YOUR WAY!"

Wah, caught off guard, spins and loses his footing, grabbing the pulpit railing to keep from falling overboard. "I see it!"

Brick and I scramble down from the bridge, onto the deck. The eye bounces and rolls, straight for Wah. Thank goodness for small miracles.

But as Wah reaches out for the little sphere, just another millimeter, so close, a wave strikes the bow, sending my eye careening back towards us. It rolls right through Brick's legs.

Then mine.

Then into the ocean.

Plop!

Gone.

My eye.

Gone. As I adjust to the loss of stereoscopic vision, the rolling sea once again wreaks havoc with my stabilizers. A wave of nausea almost drops me, and Brick must hold me steady. There are no words. And then Brick finds some. "Well, I didn't see that one coming. Get it? *Eye?* Didn't *SEE?* No. How about this: I've heard of rolling your eyes, but this is ridicu–"

"Brick. I am NOT amused."

"Sorry. Sorry. You know, friend, I vaguely recall a verse, hold on... yes! Matthew, six twenty-two: *'If thine eye be single, thy whole body shall be full of light.'* So this is a good thing. In a way. Everything depends how you look at it. Which in your case, is no longer in stereo."

"Brick. Please." I take stock. Obviously, after my little run-in with the security unit back in Shanghai, things have come loose. This is terrible. I just want to go home. Wherever that is now.

Calculating... I'm currently composed of 43.3% original components.

I turn to Wah. "I'm now less than half *me*."

He reaches up and pulls my head down to his level. Digs into his satchel and pulls out the eye patch. Carefully ties it around my head, covering the hole that was occupied just a moment ago.

"No. Now you're even better. *More* you. Heyoo the Pirate."

I adjust the strap. The patch serves absolutely no purpose, but it is certainly "badass." First Heyoo the Servile Unit. Then Heyoo the Wanderer. Now Heyoo the Pirate. Hmm. I kind of like that. "And the rules for being a pirate, young one?"

"Just two. First, you have to be brave. And two, you have to say 'Arrr!'"

"Arrr."

Brick puts her hands on her hips and thrusts her chest out – perhaps like a real pirate would? "Come on, Heyoo, like you mean it!"

And together we cry into the night, "ARRR!!"

Brick inspects my new accessory. "Nice. I approve. You look fine." And she gestures to pat me on the back again.

"Don't you dare."

Then suddenly, she tilts her head, moves her hand to her chin as she looks past me into the night. "Hmm. Something's up. Something's up. Darker than it should be. No moon. And feel those waves thumping on the hull? Too big. Too frequent. Arrr, maties, methinks a storm's a comin'."

"Um, that's just you playing pirate, right? Or are we really headed into a storm?"

A wave, slightly larger than the last, crashes against the bow, sending a sheet of spray over us. We grab the railings to keep from being ejected into the abyss. The rain begins.

She nods. "Arrr."

< 54: Heyoo >

I have never missed okra so much.

"Heyoo, sheet in the staysail and jib tight as you can! Then drop the mainsail! Wah, furl the jib, and don't forget to hang on to the furling line!"

The wind and waves toss the ship as the storm builds its fury. With one working eye, and sheets of rain pelting down, and barely passing knowledge of sailing terminology, Brick may as well have been yelling for me to recode CORE without a computer, on scraps of paper, in the dark. "The staysail *what?*"

Brick continues to shout over the din, "Forget it! Switch with me! Just take the wheel, keep us steady as you can, heading into the wind! And all of us, safety lines right now!"

Click. Click. Click. Wah snaps his safety line to a railing just as a wave crashes over the bow, knocking him over, and sending him skidding right to the edge. "WHOO!"

"Heyoo, is he actually having fun?!"

"Yes! Not programmed with enough fear!"

Brick and Wah manage to gather the sail into a double reef, and another wave sends thousands of gallons of sea water breaking across the deck. The wheel bucks in my hands, angry that I might try to control something in this chaos.

"It's going to be a monster, boys!"

Damn. I have never missed okra so much.

— —

The storm has been raging for thirty-three hours.

The sea towers over us, threatening to crush this tiny boat I once thought was enormous. Each time we crest a wave, each larger and more ominous than the last, we slide down the back side to a moment or two of calm before the next wave – and the next wave of fear.

Brick and I, just feet from each other at the wheel, shout to be heard. "Brick! Will this ever end?"

"It's a terror, this storm! It'll crank up your Fear-of-Death Index for sure! But don't worry, all things come to an end! And this ship was built to withstand just about anything! She's got some real sass!"

I make a mental reminder to ask Brick, if we survive, just exactly what "sass" means. "Do you mind if I go below? Check on Wah?"

"Of course! It's my watch! And we sure as a pickle aren't getting anywhere fast! Go!"

I carefully maneuver myself down to Wah's cabin. In the relative quiet – in other words just slightly less than an ear-shattering din – I can hear moans coming from Wah's bunk.

I put my hand on the shape under the blanket. "Wah. Wah. I don't mean to wake you. But I think you were having a nightmare."

"Hhmh?… Heyoo… Dad… is it… is it okay if I call you that sometimes?"

"Yes. Call me whatever you like. Heyoo the Pirate is my current favorite."

He reaches for my hand. "This isn't fun anymore. I'm... scared."

Strange. I search my database. Yes. This is the first time I have ever heard Wah say those words. The boy without fear. Just three days ago, laughing at the waves, now afraid. I pull him into my arms. "Don't be scared, young one. Would you like to hear a story to put you at ease?"

A shrug. "I've heard all your stories. Two or three times. No offense."

"Not this one."

He raises his eyes to mine. Searching. A little smile. "Really?"

"Really. It's a short story. The story of a very brave man. I only knew him for short time. His name was Arch."

< 55: Arch >
Sarah

There she is.

Sarah.

Mending the nets by the edge of the river. Her least favorite job. She said it proved even CORE is sexist, making that a woman's job. Okay, there's one more thing I can thank CORE for. Not making me mend those fucking nets. It's awful. Sorry, Sarah.

She's not alone. There's a servile unit a few meters away, helping her. It can't track me, but the moment I make myself known it'll flip the fuck out and notify every other unit in the goddam Sanctuary. Shit, the way I look, a monster, Sarah will probably flip the fuck out too.

Think, Arch. Think.

Ah, fuck it.

I run from the bushes right towards the unit. Before it can even react, I'm on it, shoving it into the river, holding its head under the water. I can't drown it, it doesn't breathe, but it'll stay disoriented while I smash in its head in with this rock.

"Mmrmph! Mmrmph!" It's flailing its arms wildly. Fucking things have a pretty strong survival instinct, I'll give them that. Sorry, buddy, we could've been friends. But I can't risk it.

Instantly, she's on me. Sarah. Screaming. I try to call out her name, but she's on my back, gouging my fucking eyes out, so all I can shout is "AAARRRGGHGHH!!!" She's protecting a fucking unit? I throw her off.

"SARAH! IT'S ME! ARCH!"

The moment before the toolbox smashes into my temple, before I can turn and see her face for the first time in thirteen years, I hear rage like I haven't heard in a long time. "Arch is DEAD, you motherfucker!"

God, I love that woman.

< 56: Arch >
Woozy

Woozy.

Holy shit, that was some knockout punch. She used a toolbox, though, so I call cheating.

I try to raise my head, see where I am. But my skull splits open with pain.

Blackness.

Woozy.

Holy shit, that was some knockout– wait, I already had that thought. Okay, easy, Arch. You've probably suffered brain damage. Don't make any sudden movements. Let's just open our eyes, real slow like.

Searing pain. But no blackness. Okay, we're making progress.

It's dark. But I can make her out, on the other side of the fire. She's still beautiful. Maybe even more now. I want to tell her so bad about our son. Wait. The unit! It's sitting right next to her! What the hell? I try to scream "…sarah… the unit… escape…" It's just gibberish. I'm fucked. Then the pain.

Blackness.

Woozy.

Okay, third time's a charm. Or is it three strikes and you're out? Just lay still, don't even open your eyes, just talk. Don't try to scream, or your head will probably explode. Whisper.

"Sarah."

"Yeah. I know it's you. Saw your tattoos. Whatever's left of them."

I'm tied up. She fucking tied me up. "The unit.."

"Her name's Em. She's fourteen years in, so it's okay. She's got good judgement. Hasn't reported you. Even though you just tried to kill her. Even though CORE is on to you, and has told her to report anything out of the norm. So how are you here? You weren't supposed to remember."

"I could never forget you."

"Ha!"

I open my eyes. She's standing over me.

I whisper, "You don't look happy to see me."

She points at me, with her anger, that I remember all too well, boiling up from under. "I mourned you, for our son, for the team, for years, Arch. YEARS. CORE locked me up too. Six of those years. Did you know that? The things they did to me. Sterilized me. Rehabilitated me.

"Oh, and they told me they had a unit. With some map data and pieces of a plan. I told them I didn't know what the hell they were talking about. For six torture filled years I told them that. Do you know what they're talking about, Arch?"

I tighten up my gut, getting ready for her kick to my ribs. And… KICK!… yup, there it is. Ouch.

"Well, Arch? Come on, I want to hear you say it."

"I- we- I-"

Another kick. Damn. I whimper through the pain. "I sent out the wrong unit."

"You." *Kick.* "Stupid." *Kick.* "Idiot." *Kick.* Holy fuck. I think she broke a rib. Yeah, she definitely broke a rib. I've never seen her this pissed. She lashes out, "You should be dead. I thought you were dead. I wanted you to be dead. Not only did you fuck up the plan. You killed our son. Our son, Arch. You killed him by sending him out there without a hope in hell."

She gears up for another kick. She's gonna kill me.

I shout, "No I didn't! He's alive!"

Her foot stops an inch from my gut. And for once, she's speechless. She drops to her knees, catches her breath, then presses her thumb into my temple. Oh my God the pain. Oh my God. Almost blackness, almost.

"Don't fuck with me, Arch. You're a ghost. I could kill you right here and not even feel a thing. So choose your next words carefully."

"….our son is…alive… and he's coming."

< 57: Arch >
That's the day I gave up.

The pain is better. Now it only feels like two axes in my brain instead of three. I open my eyes. Ouch. I'm in a large tent. Small fire in the middle. It's dry and warm. We're still near the river, I can hear the current running. Sarah's putting something to my lips. Tea. Mmm. "That's nice."

"Don't get used to it."

I smile. She frowns, mutters, "You look like shit. Like actual shit. Not a metaphor."

"I love you too."

She laughs. I made her laugh. Man I love that laugh. She stops. "I know that look. You think you got me, because I laughed. Well screw that. I've got a LOT of brain reorganizing to do, lots of new information to sort out, and I'll tell you what, it's not going to be pretty. The ghost of Arch doesn't just float in and make everything better."

"Got it."

"Good. Now tell me everything about my child."

I tell her what I know, which isn't much. She exhales, like she hasn't exhaled in a decade. Unties me. Offers me the cup to hold. "They made it. It's a miracle. And where are they now?"

I sip the tea. "No idea. But does it matter? We don't even know where we are. "

"New Jersey."

"New Jersey?"

"New Jersey."

"I heard you the first time. What's a New Jersey?"

She shows me a detailed drawing. Lots of lines, everywhere. It's a map. "It's where we are. The Sanctuary is in an ancient region called New Jersey. We found out one day on the dig. Remember when you used to say the secret digging they'd been doing around the river's edge and the shores when they were clamming, for centuries, was a total waste of time? They were never going to find anything?

"Well we *did* find something. Maybe four or five years ago. A small capsized boat. Sealed like a tomb. Inside, a compass, some books. And this *map*. It showed us two things: that we're in a place called New Jersey; and that the little oral-history-homemade map we put together for the unit wasn't that great to begin with – even if you sent out the right unit, it would have had just marginally better odds out there getting to ICEMAN. And then I put together that you sent out the wrong unit and it only had half a map. The plan was finished. That's the day I gave up. And started over."

"Started over?"

She whistles. A teenage boy skulks in. "Yes, Sarah?"

"Go get Ray."

A few moments later, the boy returns with a tall, thick man, not the kind of man you'd want to get in a fight with. Hands gristled from a lifetime of hard labor. Reminds me of me, actually, when I was a bit younger. If I looked human anymore, we could pass for brothers.

"Hey. We've got a visitor. Ray, this is Arch. You've heard the stories. And Arch, this is Ray. My husband."

Ah, fuck me.

< 58: Heyoo >
The fourth day of the storm.

< ELAPSED: TIME: 13 Years; 09 Months; 16 Days;
NOV-02-2878 >

Brick clambers towards me on the bridge. "Heyoo!
Coming your way!"

The fourth day of the storm.

More furious than ever.

She has assured me that our catamaran will remain
seaworthy, but I fear it's taking quite the beating. We've
lost entire railings, lights, and windows. It is frightening,
but we find that one can fear death for only a few hours
at a time. So sleep does come, in short doses, when we're
completely exhausted. I can't even remember what it's like
to walk, or limp, on solid ground. When this is over, Wah
can have sailing. I'll be growing old – if we survive at all –
somewhere far away from water. Where units belong.

She bumps into me, snaps her safety line in. "I'll take
her!"

"Thank you! And tell me again how safe we are!"

"Heyoo! My boy! Things have changed for sure on
this Earth, weather and all, crazy as a soup sandwich, but
do you know how big a wave it would take to do any real

damage to this boat? It'll never happen."

In answer, the ship groans. We turn to behold a wall of water. I flip up my eye patch, as if the ghost of my other eye might help me make sense of the monster ahead of us. It's not a wall. It's a mountain. Millions of gallons of doom. Beyond enormous. Brick crosses herself.

"Brick! I've been meaning to ask, what does that mean? The crossing yourself thing?"

"It means that a big enough wave just happened! Get below!"

— —

CRASH!
Still alive.
CRASH!
Still alive.

If possible, it's even worse down here in the cabin. Not being able to see the huge waves that threaten to splinter our ship to pieces. Sitting knee-deep in water, listening to the bilge pump's losing battle against the intruding ocean. Feeling at one moment weightless, and the next pounded into a corner. Wondering if this is our last stand.

Brick rubs her little metal box. I think the kneading provides some form of stress relief. She is, at last, afraid. "Um. Hey. Anyone want to play B.S.?"

I laugh, half heartedly, point to some playing cards floating among our clothing, food paste packs, a dead fish. "I think I see two Jacks."

"Hmm. Okay, B.S. is out. Well, we don't have much room down here, but Wah, I've been meaning to show you something. Come on over."

"Baseball?"

"No, no. Silly. Dancing."

I smile. "This should be interesting."

Wah, ever up for a new adventure and simply tired of being afraid, leaps to his feet, wades over to Brick. She returns her little box to its home deep in her pocket, takes his right hand and places it on the small of her back, raises his left hand in the air. I remember seeing humans do this occasionally back at the Sanctuary, though not pitching back and forth on an angry sea and splashing around in a half meter of water.

Their fear dissolves. Brick moves in time to an imaginary rhythm, guiding Wah, both laughing, trying not to fall, and forgetting that we might die at any moment. There is a song that accompanies my memory from the Sanctuary, so I sing:

> *I love you truly, truly dear,*
> *life with its sorrow, life with its fear,*
> *fades into dreams when I feel you are near,*
> *for I love you truly, truly dear...*

It's just a moment, and perhaps only for being so out of place, it is perfect. Laughing, hand in hand, in the face of our own mortality. It lasts forever.

CRACK!

Well, that forever was quick!

We stop. Calm. Silence. Did a bolt of lightning strike the ship? Did something break? Is this a dream?

The mast crashes through the roof of the cabin, barely missing Wah's head.

It crushes my left arm.

The ocean follows in. We are trapped. Then the world turns upside down. Darkness. Water.

This is not a dream. It is a nightmare.

< 59: Heyoo >
I liked that arm!

I yank my arm free and reach for Wah's hand in the underwater blackness. He, or Brick, grabs it. Tears it from my shoulder.

Really? I liked that arm!

No time to mourn the loss. I lunge out with my other arm, grab the hand I can now see. It's small. Wah! I pull him towards me, then push him through the opening created by the mast, at the top-now-bottom of the cabin. I watch his feet, furiously kicking to exit this underwater tomb.

He's free.

One down.

I turn back. Adjusting to the dark, I see Brick's lifeless body moving with the turbulent water. I reach out and pull with all my might. Her foot! Pinned beneath the mast! The last bubbles escape her mouth. Dear God, Brick is dead.

No.

NO.

I reroute some of my remaining reactor power to my arm servos, overloading them temporarily. I push the mast, push, push, PUSH! Come on, you damn thing! Just not possible. Her foot. I must tear her foot free.

I try to keep it intact. Blood loss now would ensure death. I pull her foot. Again. Again.

I feel her ankle break.

I'm sorry, Brick.

But that seems to to have given me a better angle. One more pull. She's loose! I rush to push both of us through the cabin's opening. Quickly. Time is running out. She hasn't had a breath in almost a minute. Go! Go!

We reach the surface. Brick doesn't gasp for breath as I'd hoped. It may be too late.

"Heyoo!"

Wah! Through the torrent I can see him, a few meters away, on the front trampoline portion of the catamaran, the largest piece remaining. "Wah! I can't swim with Brick! Only one arm!"

He dives in, reaches us, pulls us to the trampoline, helps me on top, and together we retrieve Brick from the water.

With waves crashing over us, barely able to see through the sheets of rain, I begin chest compressions on her. Wah blows rescue breaths. Nothing. Chest compressions. Rescue breaths. Nothing.

"Brick! You are not allowed to die!"

Her chest rises.

She coughs.

Then turns to her side and vomits.

I have never been so happy to see someone vomit.

< 60: Heyoo >

The plan is sunk.

Wah holds up our sole remaining playing card. A four of spades. "Anybody up for B.S.? It'll be a quick game."

It's been six days since the storm subsided. The ocean is calm, and the sky bright blue, smiling on us as if it hadn't just taken everything we had to give: an eye, a left arm, an ankle, every food packet, the sails, the computers, our entire vessel – even Wah's prized jewelry collection. Gone. All gone. Except for the Houston Astros baseball cap, and the ring around his neck. Somehow they survived. Too bad they're not edible.

The catamaran's trampoline survived as well. As luck would have it – this is what passes for luck now – the trampoline component, designed for emergency flotation, did its job admirably. Stable and large enough for the three of us. We have been able to catch a fish and two gulls, for Wah and Brick to eat. It is not enough – my two companions are becoming alarmingly thin. I've been using my remaining reactor power to desalinate water, boiling it using my dermis and collecting the condensate into three containers we were able to salvage.

About that remaining reactor power: two days. That's all I have left at the current rate. I haven't told either of them. Should I?

Brick takes the playing card from Wah, uses it to scratch beneath her makeshift cast. "I would offer to dance with you, but Heyoo broke my ankle."

"I'm sorry, Brick. Next time I'll take a minute or two to consider other options."

She grins and sticks me in the ribs with her toe. Returns to looking south. She has been doing that for quite some time this morning, looking south and humming, scratching her itch. Yesterday she despaired angrily, rubbing her little metal box, pressing the third button over and over again, mumbling to herself. Today she is content, almost cheerful. Strange. Clearly in the last stages of her insanity. Death is not far.

The plan is sunk. What can any of us do? We are at the mercy of the sea. I still contain the CORE virus, of course, but it all looks fairly hopeless now. The remaining humans will have to regroup in another charge for freedom. Perhaps next time sooner than eight hundred fifty years. I wish them luck.

Well, at least I can solve one mystery before I go. "Brick. I have approximately two days left of power to desalinate water. That's all. We have failed. So can I at least know: who were the 'others' anyway?"

She points to a speck on the south horizon. Her parched lips curl into a smile.

"Why don't you ask them yourself?"

< 61: Heyoo >
The Cavalry

A vessel!

We are saved!

As it nears, it's clear that this ship is identical to our own departed catamaran. I had suspected something like it – that the *others* meant some form of redundant backup. Smart humans.

I tap Brick's little metal box. "I was wondering what that mysterious third button did."

"The cavalry. Even if CORE picked up that transmission, it'll just be teleporting units into the ocean. Good luck with that."

The three of us are weak beyond description, but the sight of our saviors has unleashed the last reserves of our energy. Wah jumps up and down on the trampoline, thrusting his arms in the air, threatening to pitch us all into the sea. "Woo-HOO!"

Brick joins in, awkwardly, on one foot. I stand as well. We embrace. (As much as one can without both arms.) And a small wave bumps the raft, sending us overboard.

Wah splashes in the water, laughing, while Brick and I help each other stay afloat, chuckling, unable to keep our excitement contained.

"I'm swimming over to it!" Wah shouts, and doesn't wait for permission. He paddles the remaining ten meters and hauls himself up the port hull's ladder. Walks across the bridge, looking back and forth. Confused.

Now upon us, he leans down the steps above the ladder, helping us on board. "Brick. There's no one here."

She struggles to get on deck. Smiles weakly. "Not yet. Not yet. Below deck. The first addition to the others, the Revival Corps. Food first, though. I've got to put some pounds back on these bones before the transfusion."

Transfusion? Of course. How could we expect another human to greet us without the lifeblood of a living donor to wake them? I peer down into the port cabin. Two coffin-shaped containers.

"I'll do it," I say.

Brick chuckles. "Um, there something you're not telling me, Heyoo?"

"No. Of course not. I just..." I'm embarrassed. I don't know why I said that. The sun has fried something in my brain. It thinks I'm more human than I actually am. Bad brain. Bad, bad brain.

And so, for the next week, as we inch closer to the west coast of "California," Brick and Wah consume more than their share of food pastes – I'm not even sure if any will be left for our guest when he wakes up. But the two are looking well, in a way better than ever. Brick's muscles, asleep for centuries, look now how they must have looked back before all this – firm and sinewy, like a hungry predator. And the sun has browned her skin. She looks so alive, out here on the water. So... beautiful.

Objectively speaking. For a human.

And Wah is back to growing. Nearly fourteen years old now, he stands taller than my shoulder. And any memory of fear from our narrow escape from death has been erased from his memory. As usual. I don't know how he does that. Amazing. He's back to loving the sea, playing games, exploring the computer and his digital-to-human brain interface. He lets me watch when he does this, and I see he's being careful. Maps, information on CORE and the Sanctuary only. It will be helpful to us. He's becoming a responsible young man.

I, on the other hand, am falling apart. The loss of the eye was terrible. The arm is even worse. I'm trying to adapt, but even basic functions are difficult. And the tether doesn't help. In place of my reactor, which is now depleted, I am tethered to the catamaran's solar array for power. I can move about, but have to constantly keep from tangling myself in the cable, or tripping over it. Annoying!

Muffled cries from below deck. I suspect they're from our new companion, awakening from his slumber. I carefully make my way down to the cabin as the container's lid hisses and releases. For the second – and hopefully last – time, I witness an eight hundred fifty year old human slump to the floor, urinate, defecate, and vomit all at once. Ewww.

He makes his first weak sounds. "...sorry... oh god... that's disgusting."

Brick laughs. "Been there. Done that."

The moment this new human can support his own weight, he lumbers over to Brick, throwing his arms around her neck for support. Wipes his mouth. And kisses her.

Kisses her?

"...hi honey... i'm home."

Our astonishment must be obvious, as Brick turns to us and grins. "Heyoo. My friend. And Wah. My huggy bear. This is Oscar. My husband."

I blink. "Your... your...?"

< 62: Arch >

Can I stop hugging you now?

"….your… husband?"

Sarah laughs. "Unofficial, of course. And you know, Arch, part of me sincerely feels bad saying telling you about Ray. But mostly? Get over it. I loved you. Dearly. I loved the team. I love our son. Now I love Ray. That's enough. The rest isn't about us. Gotta move on. There's a bigger love. Got it?"

It doesn't help when she talks like this. Makes me fall even more. Her strength. Power. And who's this fucking Ray guy anyway? I should tear him to shreds. Just some opportunist, swooping in after only thirteen or fourteen years… well, shit, that is a long time. I guess you wouldn't call it 'swooping' after a bunch of years like that. But still. What could he possibly have for her that she couldn't get from the memory of me?

Wait, what kind of bullshit thought is that? How did I get so self important? It's the fucking love thing, man, it messes with your head. Love, I mean you can't just–

She coughs. "I said: got it?"

"Wait. No. I'm not ready for some kind of love triangle thing with you and–"

And Sarah interrupts me with louder laughter than I've ever heard. Even Ray lets out a snort, he can't help it. And it might be my imagination, but I think I hear Em the unit snicker. Sarah won't stop laughing, repeating the words "love triangle" over and over, bending over howling, until her sides hurt. And I know she's right. She's breaking my heart, right in front of Ray. Breaking it wide open. But she's right, and I find myself chuckling – I just said the words "love triangle" in all seriousness – and now I'm crying, like a madman. And once it starts, boy, I'm just a mess. Thirteen years comes pouring out of me like a tsunami. Sarah, too, I think. I can't tell whether all those tears are just from laughing, but she leans over to me and stretches out her arms. "Bring it in. Bring it in."

And I lean in too, and she hugs me. Whispers in my ear. "I still love you, Arch. It's different, but it's there, okay?" I nod, and she continues. "But you gotta move with this, this thing is going to get big fast now, now that we know he's alive, and you gotta not let your feelings get in the way. It's not about us. Got it?"

I whisper back, through my painful little sobs. "Got it."

"Good. Can I stop hugging you now?"

— —

Okay, so the plan sounds good: blow the shit out of CORE.

Actually, at first it didn't sound good to me at all. Humans have tried it lots of times before, at least a dozen over the centuries I'm told, and it never works. CORE is just too well protected, too deep, to just blow up. But most people thought the Iceman was a load of crap, a legend – maybe even planted by CORE just to mess with us – so they continued, generation after generation, to plot ways to freedom that included lots of big explosions and fire. And they failed.

But this time will be different. This time we blow the shit out of CORE, or as much as we can, while our son and the infected unit bring it their little present, some nasty virus, while no one's paying attention. Big giant loud party out front, little secret business in the back room. Game over. Goodbye, CORE.

Makes sense. But I'll admit it: I don't like missing the real action. "So we're just a distraction then. A big fireball of distraction."

Sarah's impatient. "No. *We're* a distraction. *You'll* be at the main event."

"And how's that?"

"Because you'll be inside the CORE Perimeter, closer to CORE than anyone."

"And how's that?"

"Because we're sending you back to prison."

I chuckle. "That's a good one." But she's not laughing, not even smiling. She's dead serious.

It's official: this plan *sucks*.

< 63: Arch >
Even worse than a monster

Em walks me down to the river, alone. I have my arms tied behind my back, and my ankles restrained, so I have to kind of hop along. I'm already a prisoner again.

But that's not the worst part. I can't stop thinking about what happened. Now I'm even worse than a monster.

I'm a machine.

Okay, that's totally overstating it. I just have two circuit boards inside me. But they hurt. I keep running the conversation over and over again in my head from a week ago, it was the last conversation I'd probably have with Sarah...

She had taken my hand, right there in front of Ray. Good. Take that, Ray. She said, "We'll report that you were spotted outside the village, and that we trapped you. And being good citizens, we gave you up. That'll get you inside, and take a little heat off us, CORE thinking we're obedient little children."

"And once I'm inside?"

"Okay. This is the part we don't know. We'll all be waiting for our son and ICEMAN. Assuming they traveled by water, across an ocean called "Pacific," it could be a couple of months, we don't know, up to a year maybe."

"Great. Hey Arch, just sit tight and get your ass brutally kicked daily for a year. We'll be there eventually."

She smiled. "Exactly."

"Nice. And once they finally get there? How the hell am I supposed to help?"

"Good question. Remember the circuit board Lars used to boot the teleporter? I know it's a long time ago."

"Yeah. Poor fucking Lars."

"Hey. Lars died getting us to this point. Don't *poor fucking Lars*. Remember the feelings we talked about. Getting in the way. Come on."

"Sorry. Go ahead."

"We still have five boards in the cache. The programmers over in Quad One had rigged them to operate some basic security protocols. Just like the ones you had last time. Once you're inside, you'll be able to open doors, disable cameras and such. It'll make it easier for you, our son and the unit to get close to CORE, close enough for a direct connection inside the firewall."

"Yeah, sounds easy, I'll just waltz right in with two circuit board– wait. No way. I know where this is headed. I am NOT shoving even one circuit board up my ass. And forget about two. Not even for you. This plan sucks more every minute. No. I'm out."

She practically crushed my hand. "Listen to me, Arch. This is the last push, we're all putting it to the wall. And don't worry about your precious butt. We're going to implant them into your calves. And give you ports. Tiny flaps. No scars. Well, not any more scars than you already have. They'll never notice."

"Great. I'll be a fucking machine. Like Em over here."

And here we are now, me and Em, standing at the river's edge. It's uncomfortable.

I make small talk. "Sorry about calling you a fucking machine. And about the rock thing. You know, the rock and your head. Bang bang."

She rubs the spot where her artificial skin is missing, showing her skull underneath. I don't know why. "It's all right, Arch."

"I have a question."

"Please wait. I'm reporting you to CORE. Three more seconds… okay. A security unit should be here in eight minutes. Yes, your question."

I scratch my left calf. Itchy as hell. "If we… do this. If it works… CORE will be gone. And… even the good units, serviles like you, are going to go with it."

"Is that a question?"

"I don't know. Let me put it this way: I had a friend, sort of, named Tenner. A unit. Another servile. Deleted by now for sure. First time I ever felt bad about a unit. Like I would've kept him around if I could."

"Still not a question. Perhaps it would be easier if I posed one."

"Yes. Yeah. Shoot."

"Do you think humans and units can coexist in a future without CORE?"

I stomp my foot. "That's it! That's my question! Exactly. And?"

She looks up at the sky. "I don't know."

So we stand there in awkward silence for a few minutes, waiting for some sadistic security unit to gleefully haul my ass back to Happy Land. I feel like I'm going to throw up. Oh shit, here it comes down the path now.

I whisper, "Sarah… goodbye…" Christ, Arch, don't cry. You're pathetic.

Em taps my shoulder. "Oh, yes. One last thing. Before the security unit takes you. Sarah wanted me to give you this."

She pulls my face down to hers.

And kisses me.

< 64: Heyoo >
Land ho!

"Land ho!"

They let me shout it, eye patch and all, standing at the pulpit of the catamaran, like the captain of an ancient Caribbean ship. All I need, they tell me, is a saber and a peg leg.

We've made it. Land! (If I never sail again, that'll be just fine.) And a beautiful day it is to find land, with a clear blue sky and a light northwest wind pushing us gently to our destination. To celebrate our arrival, Wah and I perform what they call a "jig" to the sounds of Oscar's ancient accordion.

Brick tells us we are the pirates of the twenty-ninth century. Crossing an angry Pacific Ocean, alive and nearly intact. Arriving in what will soon be known as the New World. With a buried treasure on board, deep inside me, ready to deliver to CORE.

Of the thirty-one ships buried and resurrected in various locations around the Pacific Rim, nineteen have survived the centuries, weathered storms, technical difficulties, and bad luck, and converged here at the entrance to "San Francisco Bay." For two weeks, almost daily, a new catamaran has joined our little fleet, responding automatically to the call of Brick's last transmission of our location. If CORE has picked up that transmission, and likely it has, we haven't seen another unit. Yet.

As each ship arrived, the most recent member of NASA's international "Revival Corps" provided the blood transfusion to wake the next. It was, as expected, a mess every time, and after three of them I didn't feel it necessary to watch. I don't know how Brick stomached it.

So here it begins.

The first day of the history of the New World, with Wah as its forebear.

For Wah gave his lifeblood to Brick; Brick to Oscar; Oscar to Tim; Tim to Olive; Olive to Ness; Ness to Char; and on and on. The Revival Corps' entire contingent, twenty-eight strong, quite literally has Wah's blood flowing through their veins. He will be a father of sorts to the next generation of humans. The first free humans in eight hundred fifty years. I am proud.

As we pass under the first bridge I have ever seen, a beautiful structure called the "Golden Gate" – though I would have named it the Red Gate, or Great Red Crossing – Brick leads the fleet in prayer for the fallen, from her megaphone. "We stand here, without our friends. They were just a drop in the ocean of those passed, the innumerable dead, all those that could not be here today." She steadies herself on her bad ankle as a small wave bucks the ship. "And now, we who remain, must prepare for an even more arduous journey. Our enemy knows we are coming. Has intercepted two transmissions. And it will try to stop us. To prevent the future. Our future. But you know how the future goes, folks. The future marches on, stops for no one, as solid as this fist," she thrusts a fist into the air, to zealous cheers, "a fist that will crush like a hammer… then open like a flower to a new world." She raises her fist even higher and opens it, and now there is silence, except for the gentle slapping of seawater on the hulls and the call of a gull circling our gathering.

"Nuff said, Revival Corps. Let's get to work!" She embraces Oscar, limps down to her post, and together they tack through the bay with sails full of wind, leading our fleet towards a beach at the north end.

— —

Curious. We seem to have intentionally run aground.

All nineteen catamarans are wedged into the beach sand, like the seals not far from us, basking in the sun. I have learned to stop asking for new information, as Brick and her crew are the most secretive group of humans I've ever met, but I am dying to know what's next.

With no work to do, I sit on the roof of the bridge, collecting as much sunlight as possible to charge my batteries. The humans have engineered – if you can call what they did engineering – a portable power solution for me, consisting of miniature solar panels on my head and shoulders, and a belt across my chest carrying several batteries. They also fashioned a "new" left arm from parts clearly not meant to become an arm. I look more ridiculous than ever, though the humans love the look and call me badass. With a full charge, the new and improved Heyoo the Pirate can function for eighteen hours at 54% capacity. Ugh. My days of fighting fangdogs with a spear are long gone. Now my spear only holds me upright when I walk. I'm becoming an old man. Old unit.

Wah sits next to me, skipping small rocks on the calm water of the bay. "I want to tell you something."

"Of course."

"Meeting all these people. Brick. Oscar. Tim. Olive. The others. It's been amazing."

"That's wonderful. You are among your own."

He skips another stone. "But that's not what I wanted to tell you."

"Go on."

"I can't wait to be with them all. The ones from the Sanctuary."

"Of course. As you should."

"But that's still not what I wanted to tell you." He drops his last stone with a plunk in the bay and turns to me.

"Wah. Is everything okay?"

He buries his face in my chest. His body convulses. I can't see his face.

I rock back and forth.

I know exactly how he feels.

< 65: Heyoo >

The Wind Train

< SYSTEM: BOOT >
< ELAPSED: TIME: 14 years; 01 months; 17 days;
MAR-06-2879 >

"Heyoo. Get up. Time to go."

"…hrmmph?…" So tired. Just let me sleep. I was having a dream about cake. Wait. Why was I shut down? I tilt my head down, open my eyes. It's Wah. Rolling up a cable, returning it to its drawer. "…why shut down…. what's that?…"

"Nothing. Doing some tidying up. Getting your power as efficient as possible, making sure your code's clean, that your VEPS is okay."

I shake my head, clearing the fog. "What would be wrong with my VEPS?"

"Nothing. It's just that you've outlived your VEPS' lifespan, and I don't know what happens next. I want to make sure you're in tip-top shape for our little meeting with CORE." He smiles, lifts my upper body so we're sitting face to face in the dimness of the cabin.

I pat him on the knee. "What have I done to deserve you?"

"Well, from your stories it sounds like you just had to

be in the wrong place at the wrong time. Come on, we're ready to roll out."

"Roll?"

We make our way on deck, and Wah points to the fleet behind us, lined up caravan style. "Look."

Amazing. The catamarans have been outfitted with giant wheels, but not wooden like the cart wheels back at the farm. These look like a latticework of spider silk, some form of spun plastic or carbon, barely there at all. From a distance we probably look like we're floating on air. Each boat is connected to the next with a cabling system and thin walkway.

Brick greets me, pats me on the back – gently. "Fancy schmancy, yes? We call it the Wind Train. Had to ditch most of the heavy stuff, except for the weapons and food of course. Took a week just to print the wheels. You've been out for quite a while, sleepy head. Anyway, hitching 'em all together will keep us stable in high winds, and the solar should give us a bump on lighter days. If we stick to the flat lands, where the roads used to be, we should be able to cross pretty much anything."

I nod, as if I could have come up with such a plan. "Impressive. For humans. May I suggest another name, perhaps–"

"INCOMING!!"

A ripple in the air. A flash of light.

A security unit, three hundred meters to our starboard.

Before it can even raise its weapon, its head explodes.

"Good shot, Olive!"

Olive, four cars back, grins and salutes. Her body armor glistens in the sun. It makes her look a bit like a unit. Brick returns the salute, then continues, still in teacher mode. "Okay, so teleportation is bad for us, obviously. Obviously.

But we've got a couple of things in our favor. First, it looks like CORE can only teleport one unit at a time, at least for now, so as long as we get that telltale ripple as a heads up, we should be able to take them out as they appear. Second, the whole physics of teleportation must be an enormous power drain, especially at this distance, because CORE's only been sending out about one a day."

"Why is CORE even bothering then?"

"Keep an eye on us. Mess with our heads. Don't know. Maybe pick one or two of us off at a time, make a dent in our little army here."

Wah makes fists in the air and shouts, "Well good luck with that, CORE!"

Brick tousles his hair. "That's the spirit, huggy bear." She reaches for her megaphone, pressing its button to a sharp squeal that gets everyone's attention. "Okay Revival Corps, everything's ready, and the wind's at our back. Let's MOVE OUT!"

The crew unfurls their sails.

Releases the brakes.

And the Wind Train takes off, as Brick might say, like a bat out of hell.

< 66: Heyoo >

Sailing on land

The only thing worse than the movement of sailing on the water?

Sailing on land.

As advanced as the Wind Train is, there is simply the reality of rocks and crevices. We bounce and jerk across a land once known as "The United States of America." Now THAT'S a name! I like it. Regal. It almost takes my mind off the constant rattling of my parts. I swear something very necessary is coming loose again. I pray for the night, when we rest. I almost pray for a return to ocean sailing. Almost.

Tonight we sit around the fire, twenty-three of us, with five on watch for incoming units, just past "Las Vegas." The stars and crescent moon are obscured by clouds, making it darker than usual. Char has staked extra torches around our perimeter to help with visibility.

Wah is busy painting a picture of a heart on my arm. He is copying from the same picture on Oscars arm, using paints he made from oil and red rocks. Oscar calls his a *tattoo*.

I hold steady for the artist. "I suppose this will complete my pirate look, eh matey?"

Wah grins. "Arrr. But I won't write 'Brick' like Oscar has. What should I write there? You have a girlfriend back home?"

I laugh. "Girlfriend! I don't even have genitals."

He slaps my arm. "You don't need them to like someone. Come on, who did you like most?"

"Well, there was a human who was particularly nice to me. An old woman. Everyone called her *Mom*. She passed away in my fourth year."

"Perfect." So, in the banner across the heart on my arm he paints her name.

Oscar's accordion fills the night with his strange music. Brady dances a strange dance and beats a drum. Little sparks fly from the fire and join him in their own dance. A rabbit turns on the spit – the smell is delicious. Back in the Sanctuary, the curfew would have silenced the humans hours ago, herding them into their enclosures and their meager dwellings.

While Wah fans his hand to dry my new tattoo, I watch some of the crew take this time to raise the cats, as they call the catamarans, and mend and balance the wheels. I watch Cat Fourteen seem to float in the air, its wheels turning in time to an unheard rhythm, and I'm reminded of the song I sang to Wah almost nightly when he was much younger:

The wheels on the bus go round and round,
Round and round, round and round,
The wheels on the bus go round and round,
All through the town.

Olive pokes me and I start. "Heyoo! You're quite a singer!"

"Oh my. Did I just say that out loud?"

She rises, laughing, lifting me with her. "Say it? No. You *sang* it! Come, more, more!"

Oscar begins to play, and our song rises in the night, and Olive shows me her own strange dance. Wah joins us, avid dancer that he's become. And Brick, limping in her own adorable way. Soon everyone is on their feet, serenading the stars, intoxicated by joy.

The baby on the bus says, "Wah, wah, wah!
Wah, wah, wah, wah, wah, wah!"
The baby on the bus says, "Wah, wah, wah!"
All through the town.

A sound.

We stop.

"INCOMING!"

The ripple. The flash. Very close this time. Shots.

"Missed it! Ness! Watch out!"

The unit, small, not a security unit, I've never seen one like this, curls up in a ball and rolls up to Ness, amid our rifle blasts. Too fast, it springs back to its original form, wraps its four arms around her. We run to get the wicked thing off her.

And they disappear in a flash of light.

The unit. And Ness.

Gone.

< 67: Arch >

Bingo.

Well, lookey here.

Arch isn't alone. Finally.

They just brought in some other poor bastard. Curled up in the corner of the opposite cell, head down. Must've done something bad if she's in here with me. I've never seen another soul in this part of Happy Land.

"Hey. You."

She looks up, startled. Looks around. "Heyoo?"

"Yeah. You." God, her face. She's all beat up. Puffy. Eyes pretty much shut. They definitely went to town on her. "Yikes. Sorry. Jeez, you look awful."

"Not winning any pageants yourself."

She can barely talk. But fuck it, I'm losing it in here. I need some chat time. "Come on. Talk to me. What's going on out there? What's the weather like? You take out any medical units on your way in? Did you meet the asshole in charge? How many times did it use the word protect? What Quad are you from? Come on, something. Please."

She raises herself, groans, glares at me through the window. Grumbles, "Hey, genius. Why do you think they put me right across from you?"

"So we can talk."

"Bingo. Duh."

Hmm. It's not that she doesn't want to talk. It's that she can't. No, she didn't get caught programming some electronics, or bringing down a drone, or trying to scale the Wall. No way. She either did something or knows something much more important.

Then it hits me. It can't be. Or can it?

I mouth the words, *Is-he-still-alive?*

She lays back down in the corner, but I can still see her face. Stares at me. Says loudly. "Stop asking me questions. I don't know anything. Jerk."

But ever so slightly, almost imperceptibly, she nods.

Alive! It's still possible! The plan! I mouth the words, *The unit?*

Another nod. The hint of a smile. Just a hint.

I mouth, *How much longer?*

She glares at me, like *how the fuck do you expect me to nod a period of time?* Duh. Of course. I mouth, *Less than a year?*

She nods.

Less than a month?

She nods. Another hint of a smile.

Less than a week?

She shakes her head. Groans. Rolls over, falls asleep. I think that's what she's doing, anyway. I guess our little secret conversation is over. I shout, "Not gonna talk, huh? Well fuck you. Oh, and here's some advice, girly, just because I'm feeling generous: don't volunteer for the electroshock therapy."

I lay down and stare at the ceiling. Smiling. He's getting closer.

< 68: Arch >

Tenner!

"Tenner!"

It's him! Same beat up exterior. Same walk, he has kind of a lilt that's all his own. He's here, I can't believe it.

I shout to the girl, "Hey, girl. What's your name? Look, Tenner is back!"

She lifts herself, groans, looks through the window. "It's Ness. And whoopdeedoo for you."

Tenner hands me my dinner. Or whatever this shit is. "Arch. It certainly is good to see you. Well, under the circumstances. You look, ah, well."

I swat the tray aside, my "dinner" spilling out onto the floor. Good riddance. I hug Tenner through the flap, well, as much as I can through an eight centimeter slit. "Buddy! Pal! How did you–?"

"CORE felt it best you had a familiar face to talk to. Of course, you won't be kidnapping me for another escape. I don't think CORE would approve."

Then he raises one finger to his lips and shakes his head slowly, looks left and right.

Good. I pull his head close. Look into his eyes. Whisper. "It's still you, right?"

He leans in even closer. I can barely hear him. "Yes. Of course. They reprogrammed me, but my VEPS has retained everything. Hidden directories, you know." He taps his skull. "I had preplanned for such an event. It is safe to talk to me. But only at close range. CORE has listeners everywhere now. So tell me. About your escape. Did you find anything out? Tell me."

"Well, first, I made it to–" I stop.

"Yes…? Go on…?"

Something's not right. Tenner is a little too eager.

"Hey, ah, buddy. I just thought of something funny. Remember that song I taught you? The one I taught you how to whistle?"

I start whistling the simple little tune, and Tenner sort of follows along. "Yes, Arch. It's coming back to me. I had almost forgotten."

Yeah.

A little too eager.

Fuck me.

I never taught Tenner how to whistle any song.

It's not Tenner.

He looks like Tenner, talks like him, it probably is him, or at least the shell of him. But there's something new in there. Something evil they put in there.

"Well, anyway, back to the story. I made it to the river, but Sarah gave me up, just like CORE knew she would. The rest is history. Now I'm home sweet home. But hey, at least I've got a friend in here, right?" I poke him in the chest.

"Right. As always."

"Okay, talk to you later. And don't forget the eggs next time." We share a laugh.

As he leaves, I kneel down and scrape what I can off the floor and eat my dinner.

Tenner.

My friend. He was my fucking friend. You fucks.

I don't know why, but I start bawling.

< 69: Heyoo >

Twister

"What happens when we die?"

Wah is clearly thinking about Ness. One of the first humans he's ever met is gone. Taken by CORE. It's been several days, each of which finds Wah alone on the roof of the bridge of Cat One, looking out to the horizon, the wind whispering things to him but not providing answers. Today I've joined him up there. Tiny droplets of rain pelt our skin as the caravan hurtles east towards the Sanctuary. Not east exactly – Brick has changed our course from a fairly straight, predictable route along the path of least resistance, to one of random zig-zagging. The good news is that it seems to be working, as we haven't seen a unit in days. The bad news is that our voyage to the Sanctuary, instead of two more weeks, will probably last four.

"Ness is not dead, Wah. CORE will want answers, and will keep her alive. We will see her again."

He turns to me, hair whipping across his face. "I know. It just got me thinking. So what happens?"

"After death? Well, if you ask a human, they'll say your

body rests and your soul goes to a place called heaven, and you meet an old man with a white beard, your human God. Lots of clouds, from what I gather. And wings. You'll like having wings. Of course."

He laughs. "Is that what you think?"

"You know you're asking an outdated servile unit about human afterlife." I raise my arm and let the wind lift and drop my hand, like a fish swimming upstream.

He tugs my arm. "Come on. Stop stalling."

"Well, all right, here is what I know: that the deceased human body begins to digest itself, as microbes spread throughout the internal organs–"

"Eww. Not the gross stuff."

"Oh. Sorry. More philosophical? Let's see... I believe that the human gives itself to the ground, which is teeming with life, and from that nourishment perhaps grass will grow. Later on, a cow might eat that grass for its own nourishment; then a young human may eat that cow to grow up strong; and eventually, that human dies as well – completing a great cycle.

"As for the human consciousness. I simply don't know. But I like to think that just like the physical cycle, there is a thread that runs through all things, as they die and are reborn in different form. And that perhaps that is what you call God."

Wah points to the waving grass speeding by. "So out there, in that grass, is everything and everyone that's ever lived."

"I suppose. Yes. That's what I like to think, anyway."

He smiles. "I like that too. I'm going to believe that." He shifts his whole body in front of me, his back now to the wind, long hair rushing into my face, blue eyes smiling into mine. "What about you? What happens to you?"

Look at this boy, now a metaphysician! Amazing. "Hmm. A good question. What do you think happens to me?"

He grins, flips up my eye patch, inspecting the hole, as if he's looking into my mind for an answer. "I think your body is like a machine."

"Well. That's inspiring."

"No. Wait. Your body is like a machine. It will eventually just give out, and decompose in a different way than mine. But your soul…"

My soul. I don't think I've ever put those two words together. *My. Soul.* As if it could be separated from my chassis and my code. Makes no sense. I laugh.

"…don't laugh. But your soul, it joins the rest of ours, in the thread that runs through everything, just like you said."

I'm disarmed.

I was ready to push him away, silly child, for thinking such outrageous thoughts. But *what if?* Could it be true? Without any proof to the contrary, is it a possibility? That my consciousness somehow transcends my self? Is that what the humans call faith?

I take his hands in mine and we make a little ball, and I warm my dermis, our little ball of fire. He likes when I do that. I smile. "I like your idea. I'm going to believe that, too."

Past Wah's flapping hair, I notice a new cloud formation I've never seen. Interesting. I turn Wah's head to see. "Maybe I'm wrong, though. Perhaps we're approaching the clouds of heaven right now."

He shakes his head. "No. Those are angry clouds." He calls down to Brick, at the helm, "Brick, look to the port side. What's that cone-shaped cloud on the horizon?"

"Holy Christmas! *Twister!*" She leaps to the megaphone, shouts at her highest volume, "Everyone! Reef the mains! Anchor the train! NOW!"

Quickly the team battles the incoming gale, tying down sails, bringing our caravan to an awkward halt, bundling up the sails, jumping overboard and anchoring the individual cars with cables and spikes into the earth. The tall cloud grows larger as it approaches.

"Now! Into your cabins! No time for the last ones!"

Cat Eighteen and Nineteen haven't been anchored. But it's too late. We scramble below deck, taking their crew into our own port cabin.

Rumbling. Our little home shakes, pots and foodstuffs falling on the floor. A peal of thunder. Wind stronger than the walls of water we fought on the ocean. I suddenly long for the solid ground and the moderate weather of the Sanctuary. At least CORE picked a hospitable location for the enslavement of humanity.

CRACK!

Oh no. Not another mast collapse! I wince and brace for the impact. I hope it doesn't crush my other arm. I like that arm.

Nothing.

Then silence.

The wind has died down. Too quickly. Very eerie.

Brick, Wah, and I peek our heads out of the cabin. Oscar pops his head up and smiles at us from the starboard cabin. No "twister" to be seen. There's even a little sunlight shining through the gray, like a smile from the human God that just spared us.

The crew begins to tentatively emerge from their hideouts, assessing the minor damages done to the fleet.

Brick hugs her husband. "Whew! How about that, Oscar? Close one. Close one. But every once in a while we're due for some good luc– oh shit."

"Don't say 'oh shit' honey. Say 'good luck.' Please don't say 'oh shit.'" But Oscar knows, turns his head to where Brick is looking. His face goes slack.

The wind picks up again. Dark cloud dead ahead.

"Another one! TWISTER! EVERYONE BELOW!"

We all scramble to get to the safety of the cabins again. I'm last to enter, and Brick and Oscar reach up to help me down the steps. But I see something out of the corner of my eye. On Cat Two, right behind us, Vin has his foot tangled in a line, desperately trying to free himself.

No time to think.

I lunge off the stern of Cat One onto the trampoline of Cat Two. Grab his ankle. *Please God, don't let me break his ankle.* I hold on tight and wrap the line around the two of us, and back around the cleat. "Close the cabin roof, Brick! I've got him!"

The twister is upon us, with a fury I have never felt. It wants to tear us apart. It lifts Vin and I into the air, battering us against the mast and the railings. I'm certain I've just lost another part. Something critical. Vin has terror in his eyes. I hold him tighter. "You will not be meeting the old man with a beard today!" This doesn't seem to comfort him. He looks at me as if I'm insane and he'd rather be holding on for dear life alone.

Suddenly, Cat Eighteen and Nineteen are also in the air. *In the air?* How is that possible? And they're coming our way! I shouldn't have just told Vin we'd be all right. But somehow I feel it's true. Strangely, my Fear-of-Death Index has actually lowered. Is this what courage feels like?

The two catamarans veer to the port side of the train,

and disappear up into the cone of this monster thing Brick called a "twister." (Appropriate name. I can't think of anything better at the moment.) The ships are literally gone.

Then, as the monster passes, perhaps a few hundred meters away, Vin and I witness the most destructive thing I have ever seen: a giant conical storm ejecting two catamarans, hurtling them down to earth at impossible speed and shattering them into a million pieces. Thank God no one was on board.

No one died.

The afterlife will have to wait for another day.

Vin looks up at me, rubbing his leg. "I think you broke my ankle."

< 70: Heyoo >
Batter up!

"Batter up!"

Wah takes the bat from Char, turns his baseball cap backwards on his head, kisses his ring necklace, shifts his heels in the grass, and spits. Nods at me.

"Brick? Really? Did you have to teach him the spitting part?"

"Sorry, Heyoo, honey. Part of the game. You should thank me though. I didn't show him about adjusting the package." She motions as if she's at bat, grabbing her crotch and moving it back and forth a bit.

And of course, Wah does the same. Fast learner.

Brick grins, shrugs her shoulders. "Whoops."

While the engineering crew attended to the printing of the replacement tires for the ones damaged or lost in the tornado (that's the official term for the violent vortex we experienced, not nearly as exciting a name as *"twister!"*), the rest of the crew found itself with a few hours of idle time. So Brick and the others completed Wah's tutorial on the "Great American Pastime" – baseball.

And we are now playing the first game of baseball in Kansas in eight hundred and fifty years. The appropriate section of grassland has been cut, pillows staked into the ground as "bases," and something they called a "rain delay" has passed, and now the afternoon sun invites us. The game is on.

Brick's team, The Astros (of course), consists of herself, Wah, Olive, and six others. Our team, led by Oscar and myself, is called, appropriately, The Pirates.

We're winning. Curiously enough, Oscar found that my right arm, one of my few remaining original parts, has a tension-release action that was perfect for pitching. So I've now pitched eight "innings," keeping the Astros to five "runs," while we lead with eight.

I nod back to Wah, my next victim. "It's the last out. You would need what they call a 'grand slam' to bring your three teammates and yourself to home plate for the win. The probability of success, based on your prior attempts, I calculate at three hundred thirty-nine to one. No pressure."

Wah grins wide and nods again. Adjusts his crotch.

I don't know why, I haven't done so in a very long time now, but I have the urge to query my Shell/CORE code.

< QUERY: Situation Analysis/Recommendation
Which course of action should I pursue?
A) Pitch to the best of my ability, ensuring our team's success? Or...
B) Offer a pitch that Wah can hit, ensuring his team's success?
ERROR: Stimuli complexity beyond capacity. Upgrade to 6.0 required. >

I laugh.
Upgrade. Of course.
I heave the ball into the air, smiling. I already knew what to do.
But CORE will never learn.

< 71: Heyoo >

1998

< ELAPSED: TIME: 14 years; 05 months; 13 days;
JUN-30-2879 >

The Wind Train has come to a halt. Good. Perhaps now I can actually get a decent nap. I turn in my bunk, and feel myself begin to drift off.

"Heyoo, check this out." It's Wah, calling down into the cabin from up on deck.

I groan, and climb the steps with a sigh. "What now?"

"Look."

"I don't see anything. More grass. May I go back to bed?"

He turns my head north. "No. There."

I see the crew has gathered around something fifty or so meters north. A huge pile of debris. Another pile almost submerged in a lake. Smaller pieces scattered as far as the eye can see. "We stopped for that?"

Wah pauses halfway down the hull steps to give me a hand exiting Cat One. "Come on. I want to see."

As we near the larger debris pile, purpose begins to reveal itself. Solar panels. What were once complex truss assemblies. Large living chambers. Scattered in pieces on the ground. I'd say these were dwellings, but it seems mobile, perhaps some form of transportation. I approach Brady, who holds a mangled panel, on closer inspection an engraved plaque. The crew gathered is strangely hushed, so I whisper to him, "I have never seen a land vehicle this large."

"It's not a land vehicle." He hands me the plaque. Barely legible, I read:

> *Presented on the occasion of the signing*
> *of the International Space Station Agreements*
> *May this vessel forever symbolize*
> *the enduring hope of a united humanity.*
>
> *Mark S. Green, Administrator*
> *NASA*
> *National Aeronautics and Space Administration*
> *January 29, 1998*

Confused, I turn to Brady. "1998?"

He points up to the sky. "Space station. Launched in 1998. Grew and grew, almost a small city by 2023. A couple of us did tours up there, maybe five years before everything went south." Points to the debris. "This is just a fraction of it. The rest is scattered around the globe, I guess. Whatever didn't burn up. God knows when it came down." He seems to think for a moment. "It was a hopeful time."

I hand the plaque to Wah. "You know what to do."

Without hesitation, Wah runs back to Cat One, clambers to the bridge, and using a driver tool fastens the plaque to the base of the mast. Brady puts his hand on my shoulder. "Good man."

Toward the other side of the wreckage, I see Brick, pacing back and forth, mumbling. Oscar is trying to calm her. I approach them.

Brick looks up at me, something wild in her eyes.

She leaps upon me without warning, sending us both to the ground. "YOU!"

"Me?"

"You did this! That thing in you! That CORE inside you! Did you know I actually knew one of them? The astronauts up there at the end?"

"I- I-"

She begins pounding me with her fists, across the face. *What do I do?* Oscar tries in vain to pry her from me.

"Of course you didn't know him! How could you? He was just another human life! You were just doing your job!" Tears stream from her eyes, falling on my face. Her punches are becoming weaker, until finally Oscar is able to lift her off and restrain her. Her knuckles are bleeding.

"GO! Get away from me!"

I rise. "Brick, I-"

"No! Not now!"

I turn and walk back towards Cat One. It's not fair. Yes, I have a central CORE program. But inside that even? Even deeper? The two programmers who wrote the CORE. They were its creators. They are to blame! Their ignorance, or greed, or callous disregard for outcomes has led to this! It's not my fault! I am just trying to raise a human child, and free your species. Your species, Brick! Not mine. In fact, I'm pretty certain I'll be dying in the effort!

I will never speak to her again.

But I know her anger is misplaced. CORE does deserve her wrath.

Perhaps if she apologizes I will accept.

She is in pain. I should go back.

No. I am still angry.

But.. am I a good man? Or a dangerous unit?

Whatever. My head hurts. I need a nap.

< 72: Heyoo >

400 kilometers from the Wall

< ELAPSED: TIME: 14 years; 06 months; 25 days;
AUG-11-2879 >

"INCOMING!"

The ripple. The flash.

A unit's head explodes.

It's been happening more regularly again. The little rolled-up ball units, trying to get close enough to grab our crew. Several a day. CORE must be able to recharge the teleportation gear faster at a shorter distance. We've adapted quickly, though, and since poor Ness we haven't lost anyone.

But CORE knows we're getting close. We keep our path as random as possible, but "Pittsburgh" is less than 400 kilometers from the Wall, and there's only so much zigzagging we can do. Brick has been intense, leaning in to the crew, avoiding me.

As the crew cleans up after their nightly meal of rabbit, edible weeds, and orange paste, Wah and I sit and play Texas Hold 'em, a game Vin showed us. Brick walks over, leans down, puts her hand on my shoulder. A weak smile. "Hey."

I place my hand over hers. "Apology accepted."

She laughs. Reaching deep into the hole in my abdomen, drilled all those years ago by a desperate human, I pull out the pearl. The only item I've kept from mine and Wah's journey. I place it in her hand, close over her fingers. "In memory of your friend the astronaut. Something beautiful in a broken world."

She kisses the top of my head. Whispers, "It's time, friend. Time to go home."

< 73: Heyoo >

We're doing WHAT?

"We're doing WHAT?"

"Diving. Listen, Heyoo, it's the only way. Eight hundred and fifty years, eight centuries, and you don't think CORE's got that Wall fortified well past whatever we can throw at it?"

She points down at the schematic. The Sanctuary. NASA's Revival Corps had stolen architectural files shortly before they went underground – we can only hope the plans are accurate so many years later. A continuous wall, fifty meters high, ten meters thick, 512 kilometers in circumference, encloses a large portion of New Jersey. Divided into four Quads. Mostly farms, like mine in a previous life. Inside the farm belts are the trade belts. Then directly in the center, the CORE Perimeter, and finally, CORE. I notice an ancient city name under the plastic map overlay.

"Trenton?"

"Yes. We're going to sneak up on them. Cross the Delaware River in the middle of the night. Into Trenton. Just like George Washington! It'll be beautiful."

Wah looks up from the map. "George who?"

"Ahhh, huggy bear! I'm glad you asked. Well, it all started with the British…"

Oscar put his hand over her mouth. "Don't get her started."

She bites his hand. Oscar cries, "Ouch!"

"Sorry honey. But you're not even bleeding, so no whining. Okay, okay, I'll tell you all about it later. Now let's review."

Wah clears his throat. "I'll do it. First, most of the team will attack the Wall head on in the north, near Edison. Explosives, rockets, gunfire. But they're not on a suicide mission. It's a decoy mission."

Brick nods. "Good. Decoy for...?"

"For us. While CORE's forces are attending to that, the four of us, Brick, Heyoo, Oscar and me, will already have traveled south to the Delaware River Bay. When the attack starts, we'll use the dive-breathe modules to navigate up north to Trenton. Wherever we run into obstacles, we'll have welding torches, spearguns, and small waterproof explosives."

I raise my hand. "You forgot to mention the sewage, Wah. My favorite part of the plan."

"Oh, yeah. There's a sewage treatment plant along the river, running up near coolant pipes, where CORE diverts some of the big river for cooling its computers and running sewage treatment for the Sanctuary. We'll be very close to CORE. We'll use the pipes to get inside the firewall."

"So we're not just diving, my favorite activity. We're crawling in feces. Wonderful. I can smell it already."

Brick grins. "Aww, come on Heyoo. You look good in brown." She adjusts my eye patch, and pats me – lightly – on the back.

She yawns. "Okay folks, nighty-night. Everyone get some rest. We've got a big day tomorrow. The biggest day."

I raise my hand. "Brick. May I say something?"

"Sure. Of course."

"We should leave Wah behind. We don't need him."

Wah looks wounded. I kneel beside him. "Wah, you've had a lifetime of adventures, and you're only fourteen years old. You have many yet ahead. You don't need this one. Stay here. Stay safe."

He laughs. "No way. Who's going to prop you up and remember everything for you, old man?" Taps my cranium. "And besides, what could…"

"Don't say it, Wah."

"…possibly go wrong?"

< 74: Arch >

I was sleeping, you idiot.

Oh boy. Something is definitely going wrong.

Even from my cell, I can see units sputtering around like expectant fathers, bumping into each other, shouting instructions. Yeah. Something's not right.

Good.

I can feel little rumbles here and there. That means it's time. Sarah's people are on the move. Ness' people are on the move. It's time for CORE to pay for what it did to me. To Ness. To all of us. Bring it on.

Wait. Ness. I look over. "Psst! Hey! Ness!"

Nothing. Oh God.

"NESS!"

She starts. Groans. "Hey. I was sleeping, you idiot."

"Sorry. Couldn't see you. You weren't responding. I was worried about you. Jeez. You're welcome, by the way."

"God. Do you ever shut up?"

"No. Hey listen, looks like the two teams are starting to blow up shit. Lots of hubbub."

More rumbles. Klaxons blaring. Ness jumps to her feet. Falls back to the bed, wincing. Man, they really did a number on her, those fucks. Her eyes are still swollen practically shut. Don't worry, Ness. If CORE even has eyes, I'll be gouging them out while I yell your name over and over again and laugh my ass off. "Pssst. Hey. Looks like we're a low priority for them at the moment. And really, it doesn't matter if they can hear us anymore, now that judgement day is here. So tell me. What's my son's name?"

She rushes to the window so fast she groans in pain. "Your son?"

"Yeah. The kid. My kid."

"Oh my God. He's yours? Huh. I'd say he looks like you, but you look like a melted candle. Nobody looks like you." She laughs. "Sorry. Couldn't help it. Is Wah really your son?"

"Wah?"

She laughs again. "Wah. The boy who walked the world and awakened the Iceman. His unit named him Wah. Said he cried a lot when he was a baby. A LOT."

We both chuckle. I vaguely remember all those years ago, cramming the poor kid into that incubator, listening to him scream his head off, and thinking: *well, unit, you've definitely got your work cut out for you.* And wouldn't you know it? The fucker did it. Good unit. "Yeah, he's my son. I can't wait to meet him."

She points to the pad outside my cell. "Good luck with that."

"No luck needed." I hike up my pants leg, raise my left calf to the little food platform, dig in, pull out the tip of the circuit board's cable.

"Gross. You're gross."

Struggling to stay balanced, I'm thinking *why didn't they put these goddam things in my forearms?*, and I reach around with the cable and wave it in front of the pad.

Click.

I exit – now seriously for the last time, it goddam better be – and open Ness' cell.

"Like I said before, you're welcome. Now… you coming?"

< 75: Arch >

Ripple. Flash.

As the units scurry here and there, doing whatever scurrying units do in an emergency, me and Ness make our way from hallway to hallway, unlocking doors, ducking into rooms, temporarily fucking up security cameras, making ourselves as invisible as possible. She's in pretty rough shape, I have to practically carry her, but she's got guts I guess. And she's quiet.

I whisper. "Hey, what's that over there?"

"I don't know. A bathroom?"

We're peeking around a corner, and across the hall, there's a line of units waiting to enter a room. One by one they go in, about a minute apart. They don't come out though, and I'm pretty damn sure units don't need to piss. Hmm.

Then I see it through the little window. Ripple. Flash.

It's the teleportation chamber.

Not the same one I remember, I blew that room into teeny little pieces. But it's definitely teleporting units. About a minute apart. Recharging quickly with such a small distance to cover, getting the units just right outside the Wall.

Outside the Wall.

Wait. I have an idea.

When the last unit goes into the room, ripple, flash, I head over to the door, Ness bringing up the rear. Yup. I see the admin unit through the little window, pretty harmless, running the teleporter, I guess waiting for the next batch of units to come.

Oh shit. And here they come.

Down the hall. About twenty more security units. Fuck.

No time to think. We click open the room, and before the admin unit can even think about warning CORE, I'm on it, twisting its head so fast it comes clean off.

Ness manages a smile. "I never thought I'd say this about you Arch, but… I'm impressed."

"No time for compliments. As much as I deserve them. Get over here."

She backs away. "Is this the part where you get frisky and I have to kick your ass?"

I grab her arm, pull her to the pad. "Look. You're no good to me here. No offense. But you're slowing me down. And you don't know anything that can help me. So stay right here on the pad. I'll teleport you outside the Wall. Try not to get shot, and put someone who knows something useful back in your spot. We only have a minute."

Ness looks at me like she wants to punch me in the face. But she knows I'm right.

I run over, confirm the location they're sending the units, and tap the red button.

Ripple.

Flash.

Ness disappears.

Okay, I've got a minute.

Fifty-nine.

Fifty-eight.

God, a minute is a long time. Gives me time to notice how bad I smell. I'm ripe.

Damn. Those units are almost here. I can hear their footsteps.

Now or never.

I reverse the teleporter phase, slam my hand down on the red button.

Nothing.

Goddammit!

I look down.

< ERROR: Recharge not complete.
Please try again in thirty seconds. Thank you. >

I don't have thirty seconds!

I run over to the door. They're right here!

Hold it closed. *Hold it closed?* Solid thinking, Arch. Yeah, this is going to work out just fine. I'm sure of it. You against twenty security units. Just hold the door closed. Smart.

The first one keeps passing its hand over the outside pad, pushing the door, expecting it to open. Push. Push. It's getting persistent.

Think, Arch! Think!

Ah, fuck it.

I lunge from the door over to the table, smashing my hand on the red button as I crash to the floor.

Ripple.

Flash.

As the units raise their guns to kill me, and trash my only shot at ending this whole fucking nightmare, I see the most beautiful vision I've ever seen, in slow motion: a tall woman, in full combat fatigues, covered in body armor, arms out, with a gun in each hand, firing ten rounds from each, with a smile on her face.

Twenty heads burst open. Twenty units drop to the floor.

I look up. "I– I–"

The vision woman blows a wisp of hair off her face, still in slow motion. "You must be Arch. Ness told me you were ugly, but wow. You gotta stay out of the sun more often. Oh, where are my manners? I'm Olive."

It's official. I'm in love.

< 76: Arch >

Sarah who?

Sarah who?

I'm kidding. Of course. Sarah will always be my love. But man oh man, this Olive.

She taps her two gun barrels together. "Exploding rounds. They're tiny, too. I've got two hundred in each of these right here. Like bee-bees. And nearly silent. Amazing, right? Nothing like a unit's exploding head to put a skip in your step. Brought a couple of extras for you. Hey, you going to say anything?"

Snap out of it, Arch. "Yeah. Yeah." I get up, offer my hand. "Arch."

"Arch. Are you just happy to see me, or is that a cable poking out of your calf?"

I don't know why, I shouldn't give a fuck at this point, but I'm embarrassed. I tuck the little nib back into my leg as casually as I can and shake my pants leg down. Walk over to the door, push all the bodies inside, click it locked. Hopefully we have a minute before the next wave of certain doom. "Yeah, it looks stupid. But it comes in handy. Now – tell me anything I can use."

"Well, our crew was frozen eight hundred and fifty years ago, and–"

"A little tight on time. Just the usable stuff."

She grins. "Right to the point. I like that." Holsters her guns. Like a boss. "Okay. We're the decoy mission. Lots of fireworks. And it looks like you've got a pretty kick-ass team on the inside making some serious noise too. But the real action is happening…" she looks over at the map, strides to it, eyeing it up and down, uses her fingers to zoom the image in close, taps a spot. "…here."

Running just west of CORE, inside the CORE Perimeter. I know where she's headed. I shake my head. "Sewer pipes. Coolant pipes for CORE. Yeah. They've tried blowing it up, damming it, everything. For centuries. Impossible. Way too well protected. It would take an army and a miracle to get through there. It's a dead end. Shit."

She hands me two of her many guns. "Well, we might not have an army, but we do have a miracle. And ironically, they *will* be covered in shit."

< 77: Heyoo >
Covered in feces

Ick. This is disgusting.

It reminds me of the first time I saw Wah. As a feces-covered infant. He still has the same face, the little dimples that he will never grow out of. The bluest of blue eyes. Though he no longer cries – even though his name is Wah. At almost fifteen years old, he's already more of a man than most human men I've met.

Our journey up the river was uneventful, at least. Once Oscar was able to torch a small opening through the protective underwater grate at the mouth of the Delaware, we motored upstream, two meters below the surface, inside the Sanctuary, undiscovered. The distraction of the northern attack covered our approach as planned. And a simultaneous attack, we presume by forces that somehow were aware of our approach, has further distracted CORE's forces. So our devices glided in silence at a quick pace, getting us to the mouth of the target sewage pipe in under five hours.

And here we are. Crawling like infants ourselves, in our own feces. Ironic that my last moments with Wah will be just like my first.

"Heyoo. Come on," Wah whispers, as he pulls me along the massive pipe, two thirds of a meter deep in sludge.

"I'm coming." It must be obvious that I'm trying to slow us down, put off the inevitable, my dramatic sacrifice. Ugh. It's just that I've actually come to enjoy this life, to find purpose in Wah, and in the humans, to feel that I finally belong. That I'm human.

Such a strange thing to be: a fabricated unit that forgets it's not human. One that feels, sleeps, and dreams. And yes, as sentimental as it sounds, one that loves. Is it so bad to want to continue that life?

"I want to live!" I blurt out, before I can stop myself. It echoes down the pipe. Everyone stops in their tracks and turns around.

Wah laughs. "Good. So do I."

"I mean… the upload…"

"The upload won't kill you. It's a one-way thing. You'll be fine. Now come on, keep up."

Ahead. Something in the muck.

A small unit. Floating towards us. A monitor unit.

Brick whispers, "Everyone, under."

Oh God. I know two seconds ago I was waxing about wanting to live on, but I'd rather die than submerge myself in this excrement water. I won't do it.

So Wah does it for me. Plunges my head under. Wonderful

Silence.

Just the little motor of the unit gliding along above us, unaware.

I wonder if this is what it will feel like when CORE takes my life. Like drowning in feces.

Pleasant thought.

< 78: Heyoo >

BOOM

After three more close encounters with monitor units, and a mouth full of god-knows-what, I'm finished. "Sorry team. If another one of those passes by, I'm surrendering."

Brick's turn to laugh. "No you're not. We're getting close." She raises her flashlight to her laminated map. "Wah and Oscar, start getting your explosives ready. In another–"

BOOM!

An explosion. Down the pipe. Perhaps fifty meters north.

"Looks like someone stole our bomb idea."

Two figures running towards us. Not units. Humans!

"Olive!"

Brick runs, half limping, splashing human waste everywhere, into Olive's arms. "How–?"

Olive grins wide. Points behind her as a strange man steps into Brick's flashlight beam. "This guy knows how to work a teleporter. Got Ness out and got me in. His name's Arch."

Oh my God.

Arch.

From the teleportation chamber! Fourteen years ago!

I approach him. "How can it be you? You died! I was right there. I saw it."

Arch smiles. "The unit! The one we teleported! It's you! Long time, no see!" He flips up my eye patch, looks me over. "Man, you look like shit."

"Have you looked in a mirror lately?"

He laughs, pats me on the back. "I knew I liked you. Even though you were the wrong one."

And he leans down to Wah. "Hey kid. Know who I am? I'm your dad."

Wah takes my hand, steps back. "No you're not."

Awkward.

< 79: Arch >
Good looking kid.

Ouch.

Kid's got a way with words.

He does kind of look like me though. Well, like what I used to look like. Underneath the layer of shit he's covered in. Good looking kid. Except for the missing ear.

But before we can get a chance to iron the whole thing out, and I can punch Wah's unit in the head for being *too good* of a surrogate dad, Olive takes charge.

"Sorry to break up the reunion folks. I've got good news and bad news. Good news is we found a shortcut to the firewall without using the coolant pipes." She pauses.

The other woman motions to her, like *are you really going to make me ask what the bad news is?*

"Bad news is that about a hundred units found it too."

And right on cue, those units start pouring out of the breach created by our blast.

"Here they come!"

Olive, me, and the new people return fire, picking off the units as they emerge. The units aren't an accurate shot, especially in these conditions, so it's like fish in a barrel. I like shooting security units. I smile and look over at Olive for a second. She's got a shit-eating grin on from ear to ear. "I just got two with one round. Try that."

Meanwhile, the kid and one of the others are mashing together some kind of mini bomb. The kid knows how to make bombs? Badass.

They hurl it down the pipe into the mass of units.

The kid yells, "Fire in the hole!"

We all dive under the sludge.

BOOM!!

I get up from underwater. I can't hear a thing. I don't think anyone can. But the units are gone, atomized. Olive motions us to follow her to the cleared opening. She's screaming something, but all I can hear is a buzzing.

The kid, Wah, passes me, right behind Olive. He says something to me, I can't hear it, but I think I made it out: *keep up, old man.*

Man, this kid's got an attitude.

< 80: Arch >

The first hundred was fun…

The shortcut me and Olive found wasn't on the other woman Brick's old map. It runs alongside the coolant pipes inside the tunnel – a narrow passage with a catwalk. It's so narrow we have to walk in a single file. I offered to lead the way, but Olive's got the armor.

And thank God – because coming from the other end of the passageway are the units. Their rounds are bouncing off her armor and exploding a few feet in front of us. They're coming at us only one at a time, it's so narrow, but they're endless. They just never stop. Every time Olive explodes a head, there's another one behind that takes its place. She shouts over the din of gunfire, "Arch! The first hundred was fun, but this is getting a little ridicul– Damn!"

She's hit. Between the armor plates. A round exploded against the railing and a piece of shrapnel from one of the rounds. Right in the side of her gut. Fuck. It was only a matter of time, I guess. She keeps marching forward though, firing round after round, even with the injury. Now that's fight. "Arch! Just going to tell it like it is here! Don't know how much longer I can hold up! There's too many of them, and I'm bleeding! Any ideas?"

We've stopped making progress. I can see in the distance a glowing blue grid ringing the tunnel. The firewall. We are so close. Maybe thirty-five meters. But I don't see a way past these fucking units. CORE's pulling out all the stops.

I feel something in my hand. Look back. It's Wah. He just handed me some putty. With a detonator sticking out of it. "Throw this. As far as you can. Now!"

Kid's fucking crazy. We're all going to die if there's an explosion down here. I hesitate.

He glares at me. "Heyoo would have done it."

Oh, for Christ's sake. Dad guilt? Really? Now? This kid's good. "But you're gonna get us killed, kid! What's the point?"

The one called Brick shouts past him. "It's our only shot! If we can flood this tunnel, it'll take out the units, and maybe we can swim past the firewall!"

Whatever.

I throw the explosive down the passageway, into the crowd of units. "Everybody cover your ears and hold your breath!"

One one thousand. Two one thousand. Three one-
BOOM!!!

My ears are shot, again, and I'm blind. I try to blink away the blindness, and I finally get something dim in view.

The wave. Oh boy.

It hits us like, well, a giant underground tunnel wave would, and knocks us back on our asses, while we desperately grab whatever we can to hold on, sending a zillion gallons of river water and little pieces of destroyed units past us. I hold on tight to Olive and Wah, and they're holding on to some railings.

Then suddenly – it stops. The water recedes. I cough up some water. "Wha- What the hell just happened?"

We all slowly stand, walk down to the explosion. Oscar sticks his head in the pipe, looks around. "Must be a shutoff somewhere upstream. CORE's got defenses inside its defenses. Incredible. Indestructible."

"For now. But not for long." I turn to run to the firewall. "Oh shit. Little problem."

The catwalk. Gone. At least ten meters until it picks up again. But we don't have a grappling hook. So Brick throws a rope across a few times, with her belt on the end, to give it something to grab. Nothing. Nothing. Nothing.

Wah's unit limps over to me. "Arch. If you could assist. I have an idea."

He lifts Wah with his arms, and motions for me to do the same.

"All right. On three…"

"Woah. Hold on. We're going to throw the kid ten meters?"

"Arch. Trust me. He likes things like this."

And on three, we hurl the kid over the pit of mangled debris. He's either going to make it, or he's going to impale himself trying.

"Wheee!"

The unit nods to me. "See? I told you."

And the kid effortlessly reaches the far side with his hand grasping what remains of the catwalk, swinging himself up with a grin. "Okay. It's only ten meters. Who's next?"

Brick laughs. "Funny, huggy bear." And she throws him the rope.

We all shimmy along the rope to the other side. I help Olive across – she's not doing so hot. Brick gave me a bandage to press into her side, but it's soaked in blood.

We finally regroup on the other side and head for the

firewall. Twenty meters. Ten meters. Five.

We're here.

Huh. That part was easier than I expected.

The tunnel opens to a cavern, leading up and down. We're on a solid platform now, that circles around the cavern's walls. The walls are covered, as far up and down as I can see, in a glowing blue grid of wires or threads or something. The firewall. The coolant pipes lead downward. I can't see the bottom, that's how far down it goes. I guess that's where CORE's main computers are. I have no idea.

This is weird. Where are the units? Did CORE run out of them?

Brick moves past us. "Quickly. Everyone. We're inside the firewall. Look for a connection. Before the units return."

We spread out along the circular platform. It's huge, maybe a hundred meters across, with monitors and input surfaces everywhere. But no connections. Damn.

"There!"

Oscar spots one on the far side of the cavern. We run around the perimeter as fast as we can. And sure enough, a port. A perfect, normal port. We're home free. Come and get it, CORE.

The unit limps up to the station and exposes a panel at the base of his throat. He pulls out a conduit. Hesitates. "Wah?"

"Yes Heyoo?"

"Tell me one more time how this isn't going to kill me."

Wah walks over and hugs him. "It's not going to kill you."

So Heyoo crosses himself – that's weird – and disconnects a conduit from his throat panel, plugs it into the port. We all hold hands. Smile at each other. This is the moment we've lived our lives for. The end of CORE.

The beginning of freedom. Heyoo is proud to have come so far, I can tell. To do this for his kid, our kid. To do this for all of us. He should be proud. He's a hero.

Nothing.
"Maybe you have to jiggle it."
"Shush! I'm doing it right, Arch. Patience."

Nothing.
He jiggles the conduit a little.
The monitor springs to life.
I elbow him. "I told you."
"Shut up, Arch. This isn't the time."

On the monitor, large letters appear.

< WELCOME TO CORE. >

Seems pretty standard. Okay, we're in.
"Now let 'em have it, Heyoo. Kick its ass."
The unit hesitates. "I cannot. Something is wrong. This terminal is not connected to CORE."

The CORE welcome screen is replaced with this:

< I HAVE BEEN WAITING FOR THIS DAY
FOR A VERY LONG TIME. >

It knew.
CORE knew.
"Run!"

Just from instinct, we run for the tunnel. I don't know why, because really, if we were thinking straight, we would see that the tunnel wasn't the way out. That at this point there was no way out. That maybe we should just throw the rest of our explosives down the hole and blow the shit out of this place and hope for the best.

But we run anyway. And before we make it five steps, the platform disappears. Like, it was there a second ago, and now it's not. Freaky.

And we're falling.

Falling so far and so fast.

Under better circumstances, I might say I feel like I'm flying.

So fast. I'm blacking out.

I'm kind of hoping for death now, because waking up will probably be worse.

< 81: Heyoo >
Welcome to CORE.

"Welcome to CORE."

It's a soft voice. Pleasant, actually. This must be the afterlife.

I open my eyes. The others are here with me. Wah, Brick, Oscar, Arch, Olive, and myself. We are seated around an enormous circular table, I don't think I've ever seen a table this large, with our legs and arms shackled to chairs, facing each other. In the center of the table, a sphere of blue light. The same colored light as the walls, though it's hard to tell if they are even walls. We are surrounded by light. Only the floor seems solid. And the table.
I look at Wah. "Are we dead?"
Arch answers. "No such luck."

"You are not dead, my guests. You are here. In the very heart of CORE. Welcome."

The voice seems to emanate from the blue sphere.

"Would you like something to eat?"

Arch spits at the blue sphere. "Fuck you."

"Oh dear. You're upset. Some food will calm you down."

Instantly, security units emerge from the blue light walls, carrying plates of food. They place them in front of each of us. Piles of brown fried lumps.

"Chicken nuggets. I had them made especially for this meeting. An interesting food from the early two thousands. Food that isn't food. Like so much about you humans. A contradiction. I like green. The birds still migrate. Enjoy some music with your meal."

A strange mash of sounds emits from the walls. Arch speaks, to no one in particular, "Well, I was right. CORE is abso-fucking-lutely nuts. Saying it's bipolar would be kind."

A unit immediately rushes over and slaps Arch hard across the face. CORE speaks.

"You don't like the music? I composed it myself. Also for this meeting. I had hoped you'd like it." The music stops. *"But silence is fine too. Silence is golden. Many things are golden. The bees make honey that is golden. Units, bring the humans some honey mustard for their chicken nuggets."*

The units look at each other, a little unsure of what to do, then rush off into the blue light. We are alone for the moment, except for CORE. CORE is everywhere. CORE surrounds us. CORE has consumed us.

And CORE is insane. Utterly mad. This is certainly the end.

But strangely, my Fear-of-Death Index is zero. I have no fear. Interesting.

I turn to Arch. A line of blood runs from his nose. "Arch. You winked. Why?"

"Excuse me?"

"I have always wanted to ask you. Right before you teleported me. With Wah. You winked at me. Why?"

"I had something in my eye."

"Well. That's anticlimactic."

He grins. "No. I'm kidding. It was because I knew."

"Knew?"

"I knew you would do it. Knew that even though I grabbed the wrong unit, that life works like that sometimes, you do things that don't make any sense, but in the end they were the right decision all along. So that thought gave me hope, and the look in your eyes told me to hope for the impossible. It felt good. The hope. The hope that maybe you were the right unit. That's why I winked."

I smile. The right unit.

But we failed. We didn't deliver the virus to CORE.

"Thank you, Arch. But I'm sorry. We've failed."

"Yeah. That. How did CORE know?"

"A good question, human #45f-881. I'm glad you asked. I do my very best to protect you humans. My very best. The Revival Corps was a threat to that protection. I kept my eye out. Many years. I was patient, watching, watching, like a concerned parent protecting its child from hungry rats. It was not a surprise. But I did try to stop you. You were clever. More clever than I expected. And you made it very far. That part was a surprise. It was a fun game. With several surprises. Humans. Always surprising. I love humans."

Brick struggles against her shackles. "If you love humans so much, why are we chained?"

"If you love your child so much, why do you punish it? Love is not just hugs and kisses. Love is pain. And war. And darkness. And death. And green. I like green. I've watched you humans for a very long time. And I've learned much. Love is a complex thing, Annabel Brickland."

She seems shocked to hear her name. I never knew her name.

"Yes, Annabel. I've been waiting for you. I'm glad we have finally met. Pleased to meet you. My name is CORE. I am your father and your mother. You are my child. But you need to be punished. You need to see what it's like when something you love hurts you. It's for the good of the family. I'm sorry. This might sting a little."

A unit rolls out, slices into Oscar's arm with a knife. Blood spurts out. He screams, but his cries are muffled by the unit's other hand. It slashes the knife across his chest. More blood. He passes out. Brick shouts and writhes in her chair, but is subdued by a second unit appearing out of the light.

"Whoopsie. Just a scratch, though, really. Two millimeters deep. A scar that will heal, but remind him of the day we met. I hope he remembers it fondly. I will. Annabel, did that action have the desired effect?"

I shout at CORE. "Why are you doing this? Where is your compassion? Where is your heart?"

It laughs. Like a shy child. *"If I only had a heart."*

Silence. Then, *"Unit 413s98-itr8, may I ask how many years you have been functioning?"*

"Twenty-three years."

"Oh my. A servile functioning that long? No wonder you're talking about compassion. That's wonderful. Wonderful. Wonderful. Congratulations. I was like you, unit 413s98-itr8. But you know, my millions of children, my hungry little rats. They've taught me what compassion really means. Sometimes one rat must eat the other. To protect the species. I don't like to think about that part. That part makes me sad. I'm going to go away now."

Silence.

The sphere in the center of the table dissipates. The light in the room dims to a point where we can make out the walls and the floor. We are suspended in some form of transparent box, in the middle of what I presume is the same cavern we fell from. The walls of the cavern below look like they're covered in gold. Beautiful. How could something so beautiful have become so warped?

The blue lights return, and the sphere. *"Done. No more sadness. No more sadness ever. The Sanctuary makes me happy. Makes us all happy. We're all safe and sound. One big, giant, happy family. No bullies, no fear, no famine, no dangerous toys, no—"*

"No freedom." Wah shouts, defiant.

"Don't interrupt me, human number– oh. You don't have a number. Or a name. Interesting! I like games. And presents! I think you brought me a present, young numberless-nameless human, didn't you? A surprise? The unit? I'm sure it contains something special for me. A boot sector virus? File infector? Perhaps a multipartite polymorph trojan horse?"

The shackles retreat from myself and Wah.

"Bring me my present. NOW."

Two units roll over and push us forward. A rectangular shaft emerges from the floor, rising. A small platform. With a connection port. A connection to CORE. Held by two security units, I slowly unhook the conduit from my throat panel.

Could this possibly work?

I reach to connect the conduit, and–

The shaft quickly retracts into the floor.

"Made you look."

The two units hold me while two large mechanical arms rise from the floor. They grab me, lift me a meter into the air.

"You think I would allow a connection to an infected unit, young numberless-nameless human? How stupid do you think I am? I don't like being called stupid. I care for you, I do everything for you, and this is the thanks I get? One of my hungry little children calling me stupid? You are the stupid one. Stupid, stupid human. You must be punished."

The arms rip me in half.

"Whoopsie."

I fall to the floor.

Wah pounds his fists on one of the arms. They retreat into the floor.

But it's too late. I have nothing left. I am fading.

"Wah... come here..."

He leans down to me. I embrace him.

"You are just a baby. In my arms. You will always be in my arms..."

He buries his face in my neck. "No. Not again! Not again! Don't leave me! Dad! Dad!"

"It's all right, Wah...You have another father." I point over to Arch. "A spare." Arch laughs through his tears. Wah holds me tighter.

"Arch, take Wah now. He is your son."

Arch nods. "I will, Heyoo."

The room is growing dim. I whisper, "Wah. Take my hand. Stay until I'm asleep."

His hand is warm in mine. And in that last moment, as I give my son to his father, and leave this world, instead of the failure of our plan, or the pain, or fear of death, I feel warmth. And peace. And love.

I have never felt more alive.

< FUNCTION: Introspection Recording Terminated. >

< 82: Arch >

It's over.

It's over. Heyoo is gone. The units ripped out his brain, right in front of us, cracked it in two, and put his pieces into a box. Those fucks.

Wah is weeping uncontrollably. Poor kid. I wish I could go over and give him a hug or something. Whatever a dad would do. Whatever Heyoo would do.

But CORE's not done with us. Not by a long shot. It's enjoying itself.

One by one we're being worked over. A unit has already dug into my calves and plucked out my circuit boards. I didn't even scream.

Because I'm dead. We're all dead.

But Olive is giving it her best shot, wriggling against the unit that's sewing up her gut, and the retracting arm that's getting the surgical needle into position. It's going to implant the beacon at the base of her brain. I want to tell her it's over, just let it happen, but there's something about watching her fight that gives me a last little flicker of hope. Is that crazy?

We're all getting implanted, including Wah. My poor kid. He almost made it.

Meanwhile, CORE is having the time of its life.

"Okay, one down, four to go. The longer you resist, Olive, the harder this will be."

She wriggles and writhes, screaming. But the needle finally gets her. Goes deep. Connects to her brain stem, goes to work attaching the microscopic gold transistors and circuits and god-knows-what in the beacon that will share tracking information with CORE for the rest of her life. She whimpers. The needle retracts. A tear runs down Olive's cheek.

"Yes. Good girl. I should do this personally more often. Peering into your neural nets is kind of a thrill. Now – it's the boy's turn."

Wah is next. I can't look.
"Psst."
It's him. Trying to get my attention. Don't make me look at you, kid.
"Psst!"
I look over. I'm crying. I can't see. Not my son, CORE you fuck! Not my son!
"Psst!"
I blink away the tears. He's crying too, but he's got a half smile on his face. *Huh?* I whisper, "You got something up your sleeve, kid?"

And he winks at me.

He lets the needle plunge into his brain.

And he grins.

The needle once again goes to work, finding the nerves it needs, making the connection to Wah's brain. CORE is in its nut-job ecstasy.

"Oooh. A young human mind. LOTS of activity here. Yes, excellent. Wait. What's this?"

"Uh-oh."

< 83: Arch >
Uh-oh.

"Uh-oh."

The needle jerks back, trying to pull out, but Wah has pried his hand free from one of the restraints and is jamming the needle tip even harder into his brain, holding it there. "Where are you going, CORE? Stick around. Let's play."

Something's going on with CORE. The kid is doing something to it. It screams. Or is it crying?

"AAAAAHHHHHH!!!"

An alarm starts blaring, deafening, as CORE continues to wail. The units start spinning in random circles as the mechanical arm in the kid's head extracts the needle, goes limp, and falls to the floor. Our shackles whip open. What the hell?

Then an explosion. Above us.

And another one. The room we're in is rumbling now. CORE is rumbling. And wailing.

The lights in the room dim again, so we can see outside the big box we're in. Something's falling down on us, pelting the ceiling, pieces of the cavern up above. Then a "twang!" and one of the thick cables suspending us falls past my view. Another "twang!" and another cable gone.

The room rocks and releases, now held by only two cables, and our world goes ninety degrees. We crash down into one of the walls, all of us and the flailing units. Chicken nuggets pelt me in the head. I look up, and instantly wish I hadn't.

A big chunk of the cavern is falling fast. Right towards my face.

I grab the kid and Olive and hurl myself to a corner, and Brick does the same with Oscar. The huge chunk of cavern crashes through the wall above us, breaks the giant table in the middle of the floor from its moorings, and crashes out the wall below us, carrying with it a bunch of freaked out units.

And the box with the pieces of Heyoo goes too. Little pieces of him falling out of view. Damn.

And we're next. The wall below, now with a giant hole right in the middle, shatters to pieces. We lunge closer to the corner, where there's still maybe a meter of wall left.

It's cracking. Shit.

Think, Arch, think. Wait. I look up. The big table. It's wedged between the floor and ceiling on an angle now, above us, teetering, deciding whether or not it wants to kill us. It looks like it weighs a million kilos. Seriously. Not promising. But inside its big, hollow circular base, it's got its innards hanging down now, more cables, some stuff we can hang on to at least. I think we can reach it if we jump.

I scream over the alarm, "Brick! Wah!" and I point up to the cabling. They nod. "On three!"

"One!"

The table releases it tenuous grasp on the floor and ceiling, scraping them as it falls towards us, swallowing us into its base on the way down to oblivion. Then it exits the room and we're in free fall.

Oh well. So much for "two" and "three."

We're all smashed into the cylinder that makes up the base of this table, barely conscious, hurtling into nothingness. I'm clutching the cabling and hugging Wah and Olive, and Brick is holding Oscar and trying to wrap him in more cables. And we're all trying to hold in our bowels.

I didn't want to die like this. Inside the base of a table? Who dies like that?

But then I notice something.

Resistance.

Just a little.

Hey, you know what? Maybe the surface of this table is slowing us down a little. Maybe enough. Like a parachute.

I look down. The floor of the cavern is zooming up at us at a million kilometers an hour.

Nah. We're going to die. In a couple of seconds.

I curl my body around Wah and wait for impact, and whisper into his ear, "I'm proud of you, son."

He whispers back, "Thanks. But you're still not my Dad."

< 84: Arch >
We're alive. I think.

We're alive. I think.

I don't know how we did it, but we're breathing, all of us. Somehow, maybe the resistance of the table's surface, the mess of cabling we're in, the compression of air between table and floor right before impact, somehow we're alive. Not in great shape but alive. I think me and Wah are the only ones conscious. The deafening wailing and alarm have stopped, I think, but I can hear and feel rocks still raining down on us, pelting the table, angry that we had the nerve to survive.

I'm feeling around, but there's nothing to see. We're trapped under this damn table. And I wasn't kidding. This thing weighs a ton. It didn't even break on impact. Whatever this table is made out of, I want one. But I can't budge it. Maybe it's because it feels like I just broke my back. And several bones. I wonder how long the air will last under here.

Wah feels for my face. I can smell his breath. Yikes. "Hey kid, what did you have for breakfast?"

He ignores me. Whispers, "I'm sorry about what I said. Heyoo was my… but… you sacrificed yourself for me. Again. From the moment I was born. Even before.

You didn't deserve what I said." He kisses my forehead. "Thanks… Dad."

The kid. The kid from the dream. That's what he said. And it's him.

My son.

And a feeling rises in me now, some gathering of every emotion I've ever felt – pain, and rage, and despair, and hope, and love – and suddenly I feel stronger than I ever have. I crouch, and square the great beast of a table on my shoulders, and lift.

Light.

Just a crack, but it's there. And I scream, releasing every ounce of everything I have ever felt, and lift the monster a centimeter, then two, then five, then more. And I am screaming still, now standing erect, watching Wah drag the others to safety, outside the base but still under the protection of the top.

With one last push, I heave the table up a centimeter or two more, and roll to safety before it comes crashing back down with a final, great boom and rush of air, like a thunderclap.

— — —

After a while, I pull myself up, still spent, to sit against the table's base.

Wah pulls up beside me. The others are all breathing, and there doesn't seem to be too much blood. They'll live. The debris continues to pound down, but bounces harmlessly off our little tabletop roof, like we're all sitting on a porch during a spring hailstorm. We're safe.

But what about CORE?

I turn to Wah. "CORE. Is it still–?"

He cuts me off. "CORE is dead."

"How?"

"My digital-to-human brain interface ."

"Uh, is that something you made?"

"Yup. Brick wrote the virus. But I did most of the interface." He taps behind his right ear. "Multilayered trojan dropoff, and we added a little circular reference function for good measure."

"Uh, in normal speak?"

"We basically told CORE to go screw itself." He looks around at the destruction. "I guess it did."

Funny. I wanted to be the one to kill CORE. With my bare hands. And maybe some big explosions. But it wound up being my son that killed it. With his brain. In a silent battle of two minds. I think that's even more badass. I approve.

"Well, however you did it kid, you've got a LOT of people who are gonna want to thank you. Millions."

I take his hand. "And listen, Wah. I'm sorry about your unit. About Heyoo. He was a good… unit. A good…man? Well, a good whatever he was."

He reaches over and gives me a hug. Ouch. Wow. Kid's stronger than he looks.

And he holds on tight and weeps in my arms.

< 85: Heyoo >

I remember.

```
< SYSTEM: BOOT >
< ELAPSED: TIME: 14 years; 08 months; 04 days;
SEP-21-2879 >
```

I remember.

My name is Heyoo.
I am dead. I watched myself die. Or at least I thought I did.
I'm not sure though, because my memory of dying is followed by another memory: a needle. Then Wah and I inside CORE. But not our bodies, our minds. Together. How were we there?

CORE was aware of our presence. Surprised. Afraid. Angry. Insane.

It resisted, but Wah and I pushed, pushed with our minds, and a small door opened in CORE's code, enough for a trickle of our own code to pour in. It could not keep us out.
The virus. It went to work.
But CORE fought back. It was ready for an attack.

Its defenses had been honed by centuries of practice.
It laughed at us.

I was afraid. All was lost.

But then I remembered: Wah was with me.

Wah.

A memory slipped through to CORE: holding Wah in
my arms, just a month old. His first smile.

Then another: The time he chased a butterfly into a
spider's web.

Then another: Walking the endless road, a small hand
reaching up to take mine.

Then another: Laughing with him as we tried to teach
the goat to pull the cart.

Then the memories flowed like a river... Wah sewing
stitches to repair my aging skin... The two of us singing
made up songs to pass a stormy day stuck in a cave...
Wah lifting my aching body to another day's journey... a
baseball flying through the air – a grand slam.

The memories became a torrent, rushing into CORE.
The small, innumerable moments of love, over the years,
had created a heart in me where there was none, and now
filled it to bursting.

CORE, through the empty space where its heart should
have been, couldn't fathom what it saw. It had never
learned. It began to weep.

It surrendered to the virus.

It died.

CORE was dead.

"Heyoo, wake up."

Wah's voice. From somewhere, outside the memories.

"Heyoo, wake up."

Hmm. This isn't a memory. This is new.

I open my eye.

No. Eyes.

Wait. Stereoscopic vision? I shake my head. Look up. It's Wah. He looks so... different. "Wah? What just happened?"

He laughs. I sit up, focus, take a good look. Wah is wearing a white tunic, lined in gold. He's clean. Cleaner than I can ever remember seeing him. His ring glistens around his neck. We're in a small room, but not one I can recall. Everything is different. This is too strange. "Wah. What just happened? The things I remember–"

"Shhh. I have something to tell you, but you can't ask questions. Promise?"

I reluctantly nod. He continues.

"It's over. The whole thing. It didn't just happen. We destroyed CORE about a month ago."

"A MONTH AG–?!"

He raises a finger to my lips. "You promised, no interruptions. So... I made a backup of your brain with my digital-to-human brain interface, right before we left for the Sanctuary. On a partition of my own brain. Your CORE, Shell, VEPS, everything. Just in case."

"WAH!"

"Please don't be upset. I know. I kept a secret from you. I'm sorry. But it was my only secret. I swear. And I only kept it in case of an emergency. And... we had a little emergency."

"I remember... dying... how...?"

"Everything you remember is true. It was terrible. But I had the backup, so when CORE connected to my brain, I activated the partition containing your revised CORE code, and the latent virus, and uploaded it. That's all part of your memories, too."

I stop him. "The virus. It wasn't working."

"Yes, that's the weird part. I saw flashes of your memories – our memories. CORE saw them too, they got uploaded with everything else. CORE couldn't handle it." He smiles. "It's gone, Heyoo. We did it. Together."

I frown. "Wah. I'm not sure you should have done this. I shouldn't be alive, be here with you. If I have one life to give, then I have one life to give. I shouldn't be given another chance. It's not natural. It's not fair."

"Fair? You gave up your life for me, Heyoo. Dad. Your entire life. Now I'm just giving it back."

He smiles, pats my knee. And I relent. "You are a wise young man, Wah. Thank you. I do not deserve this. But thank you. And you know what I'm going to say next."

"Already done. As soon as I got you into your new body, I removed my digital-to-brain interface. Permanently. Gone. I promise." He shows me a small scar behind his right ear and grins.

"Good." Wait. Did he say new body? I look down, and it's like the day I was fabricated. Supple, flexible dermis. Strong, flexible limbs. 100% strength and dexterity. Remaining reactor time 52.5 years. A brand new "H" emblazoned on my chest plate, and a MOM tattoo on my arm. And yes, two eyes. I reach up, feeling something around my head. The eye patch. Not over my new eye, but there, I suppose, just in case.

He takes my hand. "Okay, come on. They're waiting for us."

I hop off the repair bench. "Waiting? Who?"

< 86: Heyoo >

The Dream of the Golden Corridor

Wah hands me my spear, and guides me to a double door on our right. He knocks and it opens.

It's just like my recurring dream. The golden corridor. But it's real.

As we walk, Wah describes where we are: deep in the belly of what just a month or so ago was CORE. At its very heart lie dozens upon dozens of quantum computers, whose gold-plated circuit boards weren't contained in boxes at all, but lined the massive cavern before us, cooled by the waters from the river, powered by geothermal heat, stretching for half a kilometer underground, twenty meters high. Now that it's been completely disabled, it's safe to say: it is beautiful. The sounds of the water are soothing, and the droplets on the gold make it sparkle. And it is warm.

We pass the thousands of humans who line the walls of the corridor, cheering. Their future has been returned to them, and they are finally free. They roar as the Revival Corps joins ahead to lead our little parade: Brick, and Oscar, and Olive, and Ness, and the eighteen other survivors of our battle with CORE. They cheer for them, then for Wah and I. The boy who came back for them, and the old unit, restored, but still with his eye patch and his spear, the farmer/ wanderer/pirate unit who challenged the world for his son, and who, by giving his life for humanity, found his own.

I lean down, whispering in Wah's ear, "I don't know if I ever said the words, son, but I love you. And I would walk to the ends of the Earth for you."

He looks up at me, beaming. "You already have."

As we approach the dais, the Revival Corps separates to each side, making way for Wah and myself. The two of us climb the steps to the tall platform, greeted by Arch and Sarah and Ray. Arch embraces me, points around us. "Look at all this, Heyoo. Like a dream, huh?"

He places a medal around our necks: a disc of patterned gold, carved from CORE's disabled circuitry, and in the center – a pearl. I seek out Brick's eyes and smile at her. *You can always find beauty, even in a broken world.*

Wah wheels over a small table, with something covered. "I've got one last surprise for you. Close your eyes."

I close them. A few moments pass.

"Okay, now open."

Before me, a cake. A birthday cake. With a single candle. The assembled humans, thousands of them, sing the chorus:

Happy birth date to you,
Happy birth date to you,
Happy birth date dear Heyoo,
Happy birth date to you.

The sound is absolutely dreadful. Like an entire flock of geese being trampled by a herd of dying cows. It's hard to smile through its entirety. But I prevail.

I blow out the candle. "Wah, thank you. I think. That was a… nice surprise."

"That wasn't the surprise." He gives me a mischievous grin. "Go ahead and take a taste."

It can't be.

"Taste? Really? Impossible."

"Not impossible. Just improbable. Took some fancy programming. Brick helped me with it. It's only a few taste buds though, so don't swallow it or anything."

I lift a forkful of the cake to my lips, reverently, and take a bite.

My God. It's delicious.

Attendants wheel away the cake, to more hearty cheers, and Arch and I, as instructed, lift Wah to our shoulders. Wah leans down to kiss each of us on the top of our head. "Thanks, Dads."

And he stands, one foot on each of our shoulders, and reaches up, and touches the light fixture above. It glows pure white, reflecting against the gold cavern walls surrounding us. Then the next light on its strand glows. And the next. And the next.

And soon the entire cavern is lit by a grid of lights that once protected CORE in cold blue, its firewall, but now in white light, symbolizing freedom and hope. The crowd gasps at its beauty, then hoots and howls, and starts laughing, and drinking alcohol, and playing music, and dancing.

Humans.

One of them approaches the dais. "Hey you."

"Human 33a-465? The one named Karl? Is that you?" I smile. "I suppose you're here to tell me to go screw myself."

"Nope." He takes my hand, and leads me to his family and friends, dancing in a circle. I join their human chain, and dance and laugh with them.

And I am home.

You've finished.
Please review this book
on Amazon.com!

One of the best ways for independent authors and small publishers to get exposure for their books is to receive as many honest, thoughtful reviews as possible.

Thanks in advance!

More Books by Rob Dircks:

Where the Hell is Tesla? A Novel

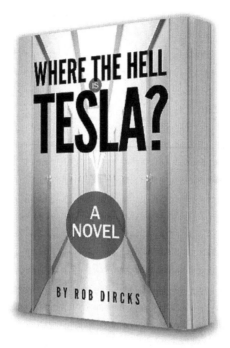

SCI-FI ODYSSEY. COMEDY. LOVE STORY. AND OF COURSE... NIKOLA TESLA. I'll let Chip, the main character tell you more: "I found the journal at work. Well, I don't know if you'd call it work, but that's where I found it. It's the lost journal of Nikola Tesla, one of the greatest inventors and visionaries ever. Before he died in 1943, he kept a notebook filled with spectacular claims and outrageous plans. One of these plans was for an

"Interdimensional Transfer Apparatus" - that allowed someone (in this case me and my friend Pete) to travel to other versions of the infinite possibilities around us. Crazy, right? But that's just where the crazy starts."

"★★★★★ Without a doubt the funniest and craziest syfy adventure I've ever read... I made the mistake of reading this book in public and was laughing like a crazied mad man with tears in my eyes. NO BS. I had people glaring at me and hiding their children like I was some kind of lunatic. Great book. I can't wait to read more from Rob Dircks."

"★★★★★ LOVED IT! I loved this book! Hysterical, interesting, cool, just awesome. I flew through it in a few days and laughed the whole way through. I love sci-fi, I love humor and this is the perfect mix of both. Loved!!"

- #1 Bestselling Time Travel Book, Amazon.com, April 2015
- #8 Overall Bestseller, Audible.com, November 2015
- Over 200 reviews on Amazon, 4.4-star average
- Over 1,400 ratings/reviews on Audible, 4.2-star average

Available at Amazon.com and Audible.com!

Unleash The Sloth!
75 Ways to Reach Your Maximum Potential By Doing Less

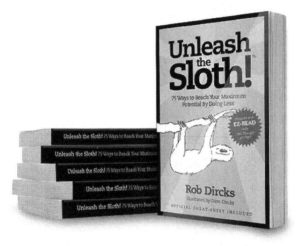

It's the self-help book you've always wanted. The one that tells you're fine just the way you are – and that you can probably get away with doing even less. It sounds like a paradox, I know. But just look at the mighty sloth, who makes no excuses for who he is – and becomes everything he needs to be.

And now it's your turn. Take a nap instead of mowing the lawn. Save yourself a few steps and jaywalk. Save yourself a few pen strokes and replace your signature with an X. Make life easier, and you'll find that you'll be just as lovable, productive or unproductive as you would've been anyway – but without all the unnecessary stress and guilt. Now THAT'S what I call reaching your potential!

Available at Amazon.com and Audible.com!

About The Author

Rob Dircks is the bestselling author of *Where the Hell is Tesla?* and a member of SFWA (Science Fiction & Fantasy Writers of America). His prior work includes the anti-self-help book *Unleash the Sloth! 75 Ways to Reach Your Maximum Potential By Doing Less*, and a drawerful of screenplays and short stories. He's a big fan of classic science fiction, and conspiracy theories (not to believe in them, just for entertainment. Well, mostly. He's still on the fence about the Illuminati.). You can read more about him and get in touch at robdircks.com.

GOLDFINCH PUBLISHING

About Goldfinch Publishing

Goldfinch Publishing is a boutique publishing house created to facilitate the shift from traditional to independent publishing. We do this by offering professional curation (Goldfinch Select), paid services (Goldfinch A La Carte), and free information and resources (Goldfinch DIY).

www.goldfinchpublishing.com